ON THE BALL!

(A Football Story)

On the Ball!

(A Football Story)

Sydney Horler

www.1889books.co.uk

ISBN: 978-1-915045-24-9

INTRODUCTION

There is something wonderful about opening up an old book: something about the life that book has led and the people who once read it – imagining the shelves it sat on, the bed covers it was read under by torchlight, conjecture on the years that followed and its eventual arrival in a second hand bookshop. So much to read between the lines.

The copy of *On the Ball!* that I tracked down contains and inscription on the inside cover:

December 1936.

With Best Wishes
to Billee
From Mummy

That British sense of restraint: *With best wishes*! Billee looked after the book and cherished it – that can be seen from the rare in-tact dust-cover (…either that or Billee was too busy kicking a ball around outside so shoved it in a box under the bed!)

But what relevance is all this? Well, it says a lot about the book itself – perhaps all you need to know. Just the sort of book that Mummy would buy for Billee – a boy's book about football, but also a moral tale, an improving read, reinforcing values of the old order, class and the civilizing structures of Empire. Perhaps Mummy even packed it in Billee's trunk before her little boy was dispatched to boarding school to beat the empathy and sensitivity out of him, with only a little, secret tear shed.

On the Ball! was published in 1926, it's author already being on a roll with football novels by this stage, being, perhaps the eighth such that he wrote.

The book is problematic to any modern reader with any shred of conscience or belief in social justice or diversity. There is a strong theme of heredity, of physical and mental superiority being innate, of social position being determined rightfully at birth. A French website describes it as his "credo of the so-called intellectual, physical and moral superiority of members of the dominant social class of British society." It goes further than that, however, and certainly through a modern lens, and probably with an objective one, Horler can be described as racist, anti-Semitic and homophobic. All this given the political undercurrents building at the time, and that the author did not shy away from racial and class tropes in his writing is enough to make you shudder at times.

There is also strong theme of physical perfection being genetic, for example:

> "I saw him as I saw him in the train, flushing scarlet when he explained that he had never played football – and yet after two appearances in the field Manners spoke of hime as a "possible" for the school colours! But – of course, I recollected now – his father was the great Vassall!. The latter must have handed down as a hereditary gift the ability to play. Vassall had the instinct!"

The novel's narrator looks on, slightly outside the action: "for this is tale of football, of thrilling deals performed upon churned turf – and with my club-foot, my place was always upon the touchline, and never upon the muddy field."

No doubt the Rees-Moggs of this world could read this novel and have their values and prejudices reinforced (except they wouldn't go near something like football for many reasons, no doubt). They could read this without any reflection and just think that the account of privilege, house-masters, prefects, fagging and ragging was "spiffing" and "topper." The rest if us can read it as a story about a way of life that should have been ended years ago, but alas still hangs on in our country – something cankerous and malevolent holding the country back from liberating all the talent of this diverse nation. Something that has led us down a path of becoming a meaner less tolerant, more unequal society, run in the interests of the privileged few, a choking of vitality that has strengthened in recent years, widening the gap between the haves and haves-not to a greater degree than at any time since this book was published. Those old school tie attitudes still infect many of our institutions: government, the civil service, the BBC and other media. And we are going backwards in many areas like the acting profession where working class kids are no longer able to make it as Christopher Eccleston so eloquently described in his interviews from April 2023 following closure of Oldham's historic Coliseum theatre. To find a way-in to acting now requires, above all, money, breeding and connections. The same applies in so many areas of our society.

All that said, *On the Ball!* is not to be read as something to get you riled or to fuel your rage against . It is despite all that a well-written story. On one level, you can read this as a quaint (though flawed) tale from yesteryear – a moral tale from a bygone age.

So why is a left-leaning publisher going anywhere near this stuff? Shouldn't such nonsense be consigned to history and stay there, never to be read again? No. Definitely not. It should not only be read but can even be enjoyed. In the first place, you could level some similar criticisms against PG Wodehouse, Sherlock Holmes stories, Raffles or many others. Context and interpretation are everything. We need to understand how people used to think – and still do, without ignoring it or diminishing the viler aspects. Plus, there is a sort of cosy nostalgia to the novel, like you'd get with watching the original *Goodbye, Mr Chips*: simpler times, simpler morality – even if you have no experience of that milieu. Finally, Horler can write about football with skill. In my blog in Football fiction https://stevek1889.blogspot.com/ I have the best cataloguing of football novels I think you'll find anywhere and Horler's works have an important place in that catalogue. He can bring something of what is a visual and sensory experience to life on a page. He understands the game and his passion for it shines through. His writing on boxing is not far behind. By way of proof, take he following paragraph from chapter twenty-one of *On the Ball!*:

> "Goal!" The cry seemed to split the sky. Hit truly, the ball had traveled like a brown bullet, wide of the school goalkeeper's right hand, and came to rest snugly in the lower right-hand corner of the net. A lovely, a beautiful goal! One to cherish in the memory and recall when one's spirits are low and one is inclined to think that life is a mocking farce.

Doesn't that nail it? Isn't that why so many of us exhibit such bizarre behaviour in relation to "eleven men just kicking a ball about"? Isn't it that antidote to those thoughts of life being a *mocking farce* – whichever words you might choose to express that feeling?

Horler's football stories are not great literary works though, despite that. In his day he was dismissed as a producer of pulp-fiction – but he was hugely popular, selling large numbers of books, particularly his "thrillers."

Sydney Horler was born in Leytonstone in Essex in July 1888. He was educated in Bristol at Redcliffe Boys School, then at a boarding school: Colston's (yes, him – of Bristol statue in the dock fame). After a brief foray into teaching he became a newspaper reporter at the *Western Daily Press* in Bristol in 1905, ending up in Fleet Street working on the *Daily Mail* and in a government propaganda department towards the end of the First World War. After the war he went to work for publisher George Newnes, a publisher of a lot of mass market and serialised fiction at the time.

He wrote in his autobiography that: "at the time I was casting around in my mind for a regular source of fiction material. I hadn't seen a professional football match since my school days but Lady Luck now led me to the ground of a professional football club once again." The match was Fulham against the club he supported as a child: Bristol City. "Directly I saw those scarlet jerseys of the team whose fortunes I had so passionately followed as a youngster something like 20 years slipped away from my shoulders as I became a schoolboy again. Then came the inspiration: no-one, apart from boys' comic writers, had ever turned England's greatest national sport, professional football, into fiction. So I resolved to have a shot at the thing myself..."

Horler's first football novel *Goal!* was published in 1920. A reviewer for the George Newnes periodical John O London's Weekly called it the "first work of fiction entirely devoted to our great national pastime" – which I believe it is (long-form fiction at least). They also added: "I should not be surprised if football novels have a great vogue."

His first rush of enthusiasm for football as a theme for fiction had waned by the time he wrote the autobiography in 1933 when he said: "I have proved from experience that the people who go in their millions to football matches are not willing to spend money on buying books dealing with their favourite sport." Thereafter, Horler concentrated on his thrillers, for which he was best known. Part of the problem was perhaps Horler's limitations as a writer. *On the Ball!* and *The Great Game/McPhee* are well worth reading in their own right. *Goal! The Legend of the League* and *The Ball of Fortune,* however interesting they are, have so many similarities of plot that you could say that once you've read one you've read them all (or if you are being generous, that if you enjoyed one then you've two more that you'll enjoy equally – people like the familiar, no?) He could not be accused of being shy of recycling the odd idea – a gag worth telling is worth telling several times (take goat mascots, for instance). What he was not capable of doing though was to take the concept of a novel themed around football and develop it in any way and certainly not in the direction of intelligent character-led or ideas-led fiction. He found his niche with mass-market pulp fiction thrillers. But to what extent did those early forays further pigeonhole football fiction into being not capable of more than *Boys Own Paper / Roy of the Rovers* fiction. What a shame that the 1912 Arnold Bennett story, *The Matador of the Five Towns* (see: https://www.1889books.co.uk/historical-football-stories) was not the lead example that set the tone for the genre.

But perhaps bigger problem was, and still is, the snobbery of the middle-class literary elite: who have always had a firm stranglehold over the publishing industry: both from a writing perspective and from the decision-making about what will sell. It is true that a love for football doesn't translate into a love of reading a book that has a football theme – other than, often tedious, ghostwritten autobiographies for some reason. There was of course a dalliance with Fever Pitch – it certainly caught a mood in the early 90s and tickled a London literary scene that had newly discovered football, finding it briefly trendy in the wake of Gazza's Italia 90 tears. But can it even be described as fiction. Isn't it more a self-indulgent whinge than a story? Does anyone doubt that it would have disappeared without trace if it had been written about Notts County, Bury FC or Crewe Alexandra and not the metropolitan elite of Arsenal? No one should be surprised – publishing is after all a branch of the fashion industry.

They say that brutes kicking a ball around on a muddy field is not art and is pointless. Priestley puts it better than anyone: "To say that these men paid their shillings to watch twenty-two hirelings kick a ball is merely to say that a violin is wood and catgut, that Hamlet is so much paper and ink."

What sells is not necessarily good, but trendy and marketable to the early thirties female on the Northern Line or the working-from-home hipster to read over breakfast at that trendy little café over a £9 bowl of porridge and a £4 turmeric latte. They will read a Hardy classic with a farming theme even if they know nothing about farming, but heaven forefend they would go near a classic like *The Hollow Ball* or *The Thistle and the Grail*, because football is for oiks. You can read a book about a person with any other job in the world and enjoy it for the story and the literature, but if the main character is into football or a footballer – then if must be worthless. *The Blinder* is probably Barry Hines finest novel, but, good though it is, it is *A Kestrel for a Knave* that everyone bangs on about – in fact it is usually the film *Kes* that people remember, and they've not even read the book.

It is often claimed that baseball and American football have inspired great novels, so why can't Association football produce a great novel? (In fact Horler drew inspiration from Charles Evan Loan who, in the early 1900s, created popular fiction based around baseball.) However, this claim is nothing than a lazy myth. As well as those mentioned, I could also cite *Papeles en el Viento* by Eduardo Sacheri, *Abide With Me* by Ian Ayris, and *Dans La Foule* by Laurent Mauvignier. All of these are as good as, and in my opinion, better than the raved about American baseball novels *The Natural* and *Shoeless Joe*. And don't even get me started on *American Pastoral*. *The Ghosts of Inchmery Road* and *The Lives of Stanley B* by Mat Guy are also superb novels that haven't received the recognition they deserve.

Of course I don't claim that Horler is up there with the best football novels, but the very fact he was a pioneer makes him worth reading.

There was a strong tradition of football at the public schools in the 19th Century, which had perhaps started to fade by the time this novel was set – rugby having become dominant amongst that class.

It has perhaps been over-stated just how important a role the public schools had in the development of the modern game, however. Back in the mid 1800s there were many different games around Britain calling themselves "foot-ball," most of which involved some sort of catching, but it was some clever chaps from Sheffield, William Prest and Nathaniel Creswick, who saw sense and applied the logic to the words 'foot' and 'ball' and wrote the Sheffield rules to codify the game they loved and restricted handling and hacking in order to civilise the sport. These rules were the precursor to the modern game and Sheffield worked with, and had great influence over, the nascent Football Association.

The evidence does not support the lazy assumptions that it must have been an invention of the public schools. Clearly they made attempts to codify some sort of "foot-ball" but it was the Sheffield rules that most shaped the modern game. James Walvin in his book *The People's Game* suggests that the "Sheffield Club was established under the influence of Old Harrovians who persuaded local village footballers not to handle the ball, allegedly by providing the players with white gloves and florins to clutch during the game." This is clearly total piffle! Such myths are just history being written by the victors yet again (this time the victors in the class struggle who can't abide the thought of a grubby unfashionable place like Sheffield having given birth to the beautiful game). You only need to think about it to realise what utter nonsense it is: a Sheffielder wearing white gloves? – to play football?? – holding in his hands half a week's wages??? They would have just kept running and gone down the pub laughing at the chinless wonders from Harrow. There is to the contrary plenty of evidence that football was played in and around Sheffield as a folk game with no external influence from posh schools in the south. It is likely that these folk games were the inspiration of the game. Of course Sheffield can't claim the sole credit – the game developed like many great inventions through collaboration and that certainly involved men in the FA from the public schools.

Horler died in a Bournemouth nursing home in October 1954 at the age of 66.

A note on the illustrations:

The cover and interior illustrations are by T.M.R. Whitwell (Thomas Montague Radcliffe) - a renowned illustrator from the late 19th and early 20th century. He produced illustrations and covers for various authors including several P.G. Wodehouse novels, for magazines, including *The Boy's Own Paper*.

– Steven Kay 2024

CHAPTER I

The Bearer of a Famous Name

Because Stanhope, and a few of the other fellows who really count at Repington, have made me promise, I Gordon Watney ("Old Dot-and-Carry"), now sit myself down to tell the story of David Vassall—of his coming to Repington, the school which all who pass through it love with a pride that cannot be expressed, of what happened to him whilst he was there, and of the influence he left behind him. I want you who read this to regard me as I regarded myself: merely as a spectator, an onlooker. Indeed, I could not have been anything else, for this is a tale of football, of thrilling deeds performed upon churned turf—and, with my club foot, my place was always upon the touchline, and never upon the muddy field. How my heart ached every time I heard the brown ball bounce—but this history is of David Vassall, not of myself.

The story I have to tell starts on the first day of the term. When I got to Paddington, I found the train uncomfortably crowded, but eventually the porter contrived to find me a place. After bestowing my traps, I looked round, and there, opposite me, was a fellow wearing the Repington cap. A new boy, I gathered, although he looked fifteen or so, but he was the Repington type—so that was all right. My qualms were soon eased. I liked him on sight—his clean-cut features, the way he carried himself, the whole look of him.

I felt I wanted to talk, although it is scarcely considered the thing at Repington for seniors to unbend—at least, not at first acquaintanceship. But it's hard for a fellow who is forced to go limping through life to put on airs, and so I handed my *Punch* across.

He took the paper with a smile, looked through it, and handed it back with a 'Thanks!—ever so much.' Just then the train stopped, disgorging the crowd, and we had the carriage to ourselves.

'New chap?' I hazarded.

'Yes.' He smiled. 'I'm rather dreading it, in a way. You see, I've only been to a prep school so far.'

I became the benevolent father.

1

'Nothing much to dread. Repington's the finest shop in England. You'll soon settle down.'

'I wonder.' And he smiled in that deprecating fashion again.

A curious remark for a fellow to make. The study of my fellow-humans being one of my hobbies, I became even more interested.

'What house are you fixed for?'

'Tadburn's.' He gave me the impression of gulping the word.

'Tadburn's! That's *my* house. The best house in the shop—although it's had a slump lately. You ought to consider yourself lucky, young 'un!' I didn't wish to be "side-y," but this new kid had distinctly gulped the word, as though it was distasteful. Why?

'Yes.' he admitted, 'so I've heard. Well, I shall do my best.'

There was something about his talk which I couldn't quite place or understand. He seemed to be afraid of something which awaited him— and yet he was going to Tadburn's! Evidently, although his people had had sound sense in sending him to Repington, his education had been sadly neglected. It was up to me to remedy that—especially as we could talk now without anyone overhearing.

'I'm going to speak to you for the good of your soul, young 'un,' I started severely. 'I'm not going to ask you the reason, but it's plain from what you have already let drop that you are dreading mixing with the cultured society you will find at Repington. Dreading!—when you ought to go on your knees in thankfulness at your luck in being able to get in at all!'

All of which, no doubt, sounds more than a trifle old-fashioned (savouring of *Tom Brown's Schooldays*), being pretentious, smugly self-satisfied, not to say priggish; yet, priding myself a trifle on being something of a student of character, I thought that the means I was using were the best to achieve my end—the latter being to instil into this new kid right away a wholesome respect and admiration for the school which we were rapidly nearing.

'I know Repington's a fine show,' he admitted.

'And Tadburn's is the best house in the shop—never forget that either, young 'un! Now, I want to tell you something about Tadburn's. Up to this term we've always carried off most of the sporting pots—cricket, and football especially. By the way, are you any good at football?'

I was astonished to see a vivid flush come into his face. 'I've—I've never played!' he said, and blushed like a girl.

'Never played!' It seemed inconceivable! He looked a player; I was hoping he was one: Tommy Stanhope and Bridges would have stood me a supper on the strength of my bringing a new kid who could really use his feet into the house. 'Never played!' My heart went down into my club foot.

'I was supposed to be delicate at the prep school,' he explained; 'all rot, of course.'

Well, I was glad he was sick about it.

'You look fit enough now,' I said; and he replied eagerly: 'I am.'

'Then you will have to play—everyone plays in Tadburn's—except me, of course—' and I stretched out old "Dot-and-Carry."

He didn't answer, but the flush on his face became more noticeable.

'Since you don't appear to be interested, perhaps I'd better leave you to find out about Tads' for your-self,' I said coldly.

'No—tell me! I want to know—I do really!' He had leaned forward, and his tone was sincere. 'Al-though I have never played, I'm interested in football.'

That made a certain difference, of course, so I took up my tale.

'Tadburn ("Tads" as we call him) is an old Oxford Soccer Blue. He has made the house what it is. He's absolutely keen on sport, but especially on footer. He's so keen that, if you are in his house, unless you have a doctor's certificate, you have to play.

'The result has been that Tads' has won more pots than any other house for the last three years. But things are looking black for this term, unless some quite unsuspected genii in a playing sense are found amongst the new kids.'

'Why?' Yes. clearly he was interested. Really, this new chap frankly puzzled me.

'Because at least half of last season's team—including four School Eleven Caps—have left. Stanhope, who has been elected House Captain, will be searching high and low for fresh blood. You see, it means something to sing small after we have been Cock House at footer for so long. You understand that?'

'Yes,' the new chap replied slowly, as though he was thinking pretty hard, 'I can see that.'

I waited for him to say something else, but he didn't, and so having done all I could, I settled back into my corner.

Going back to Repington was always a wonderful experience for me. From the first day the place held my soul. Its traditions—those revered memories which cluster so thickly around the grey school buildings—the old elms bordering the playing-fields, the different houses scattered here and there, the tall chapel spire showing through the trees like something guiding one home, the pavilion which you can see outlined from the Fives Court as you turn in through the worn wicket-gate, the gleam of the sun, mellowing everything, make it kindly, giving one the welcome of a friend:

that was to Repington to me, and my heart jumped as the train slowed down, and the well-remembered platform came into sight.

'Here we are,' I said hobbling up. 'By the way, what's your name?'

'My name?' he repeated.

'Yes, man—your name! You have a name, I suppose?'

'My name's Vassall.'

'What—?' I started, when, in getting out of the carriage, something bumped into me, something rude—something called Peter McPhail, incidentally one of Repington's proudest, if most curiously bizarre, possessions.

McPhail was a junior, but he probably exercised more authority— being himself—than any senior in the place, with the possible exception of Manners, the School Footer Captain.

'Welcome, light of my grey hairs!' exclaimed McPhail, embracing me after the manner of a Pilgrim Father—did Pilgrim Fathers embrace? I really forget. Anyway, to the open-mouthed amazement of my travelling companion, the youth, whose flaming red hair showed up conspicuously beneath his dark blue cap, threw both arms round me, patting my back with his hands like a mother soothing a recalcitrant child.

You couldn't crush McPhail unless you sat on him, so, although my dignity as a senior went overboard in the process, I smiled.

'And you have a youth with you—a comely youth if these old eyes of mine do not deceive me!' said McPhail, in a quavering voice; 'tell me, Clubfoot the Avenger, who is this comely youth?'

'McPhail is the school comedian—you mustn't mind him,' I said, turning to Vassall. 'This chap's name is Vassall—and he's coming to Tads''

'Vassall—Vassall,' muttered McPhail, suddenly serious, 'there was a Vassall who played for the Corinthians years and years ago. Was he any relation of yours?'

'I should explain that all McPhail troubles about in this world is soccer football,' I explained—and then to my astonishment, Vassall flushed crimson again.

'That was my father,' he said, speaking to McPhail.

CHAPTER II

The Cross-examination

Stanhope had asked me, and I had drifted along to his study. Bridges and Jenkins were already there, and I had only just sat down to the hospitable cup of tea before in walked McPhail . This completed the Committee on Footer.

Before I go any further, I had better make a few marginal notes about McPhail, sometimes known by his Christian name of "Peter," but more frequently referred to by his contemporaries as "Fireworks."

McPhail was a boy apart. If any other junior had shown one hundredth part of the outrageous precocity displayed by McPhail, he would have been simply extinguished. That such a school as Repington suffered its dignity to be shattered by the audacious pranks that McPhail was always perpetrating was inconceivable—until you met McPhail in the flesh. Then some dim light of understanding penetrated your brain. McPhail was unique, a law unto himself, a junior only by freak of birth, and no disciplinary power on earth was strong enough to check him. His father was a millionaire owner of newspapers: I mention this mainly as a fact, and not entirely as an explanation. Words would dry on my pen if I attempted to explain McPhail comprehensively—in the mass, as it were.

At his prep school, McPhail had been known expressively as "Ginger, Genius"—the "Ginger" being a vulgar description of his red head, and the "Genius" applying to the many sensational stunts he brought off, the majority of them right under the noses of the authorities. Stoneburgh, the academy it question, must have breathed much more freely when McPhail "passed on."

Irrepressible, McPhail had a man's brain in a boy's body. He was mentally developed many years beyond his age. Although he had the face of a cherubic choir-boy, he had the devastating mind of a masterly thinker. It was characteristic that the first thing he did upon arriving at Repington was to appoint himself fag to Tommy Stanhope. Stan-hope was on one occasion asked how the arrangement came about.

'Dashed if I know,' stated Tadburn's Footer Captain, 'the kid just sauntered in to me, said that he had come to the conclusion after mature — "mature" mark you—consideration that, since fagging seemed a necessary evil at this shop, he would rather labour in my vineyard than anyone else's. Naturally enough, I tanned him—and then made him my fag. As a matter of fact, I don't mind telling you fellows that the kid sort of mesmerized me— "bent me to his will" I believe he described it afterwards. Anyway, he's the brightest bean in Repington, and I wouldn't lose him now for a ton of dough-nuts.'

In a very short space of time McPhail had made his presence felt. He created the same sort of influence at Repington as Kipling must have done at that Crib of his. He commenced sending in things to the School Mag which were so diabolically clever that they had to be printed—and fag though he was, he actually helped to pick Tads' footer teams! That was why he was in Stanhope's study now. Making just one more explanatory and marginal note, I should add that McPhail was the recognized soundest judge of a player in the house, Stanhope himself not excepted. The whole existence of this red-haired scion of a newspaper millionaire in the winter terms was absorbed in footer; for the rest of the year McPhail just loafed and thought out fresh ways of stirring up the school—and he often talked of "running" a professional football team of his own after he left Repington. Quite a unique lad.

'Well, here we all are,' started Stanhope cheerily, ordering McPhail to fill up the tea-pot. 'I can't say that this is as convivial a pow-wow as I should have liked, gents, because—well, we seem to be in much the same interesting position as the ancient Egyptians—was it the Egyptians, you red-headed grinning imp?'

'If you refer to the coves who had to make bricks without straw, I believe you are historically inaccurate,' replied McPhail, gravely buttering a fresh piece of toast.

'Well, that seems to be our job this term,' gloomily proceeded the Captain of Tads'; 'there's Morris, Stephenson, and Winter gone amongst the seniors, and young Huish, the best left winger outside the School Eleven, is down with appendicitis, and, even when he does come back, he probably will be forbidden to play. A nice outlook for the cock house at footer isn't it? Won't Canaver's crow?' Canaver's House was our most formidable rival. This season they threatened to swamp the field, because —lucky blighters—they had practically last year's football team intact.

Jenkins, a lumbering fellow, who played right back as to the manner born, but who was slow-witted otherwise, shifted his clumsy form.

'It means practically a new team—I was telling Tads so this afternoon. He asked me had we gone through the new kids?'

'Jenks,' answered Stanhope, 'there are occasional moments when you startle me by showing the first dim dawnings of intelligence. McPhail,' turning to the fag, 'what instructions did you receive from me this afternoon?'

For once McPhail answered like a normal fag.

'To round up all the new kids and order them to report here to you between tea-time and prep.'

'Good idea, Stan,' commended Bridges, a fine dribbler at inside left; 'who knows?'

'Who knows indeed?' answered Stanhope; 'Ah!' as a knock sounded on the study door, 'here's the first claimant after Fame.'

The boy who came timidly into the room in answer to Stanhope's full-throated 'Come!' didn't look much like a claimant after football fame; he was an excessively weedy youth—an obvious "hopeless" from the start. He confessed that he had never played football, but admitted that he was willing to try—only he said it with about as much enthusiasm as a condemned prisoner going to his execution.

Stanhope groaned after he had dismissed him. 'If they're all like that—!'

The next three didn't give the market much of a lift. Jenkins and Bridges had now added their dismal groans to their skipper's, turning the study into a charnel house of hope. I was as keenly interested as any of the others, but my mind wasn't fully on these kids who meandered in and out: I was thinking of the boy Vassall, whom I had met in the train and who, although the son of a famous old Rep. and an International Corinthian to boot, had seemed confused at the very mention of football. What sort of a show was he going to make? How would he impress Stanhope and the other two seniors?

Then he walked in.

'Name?' asked Stanhope briskly.

'Vassall.' He had glanced at me, and of course I had given him a smile of encouragement. It is rather an ordeal for a new kid—and a boy who had never been to anything more important than a prep school before—to meet his House Captain and to have his antecedents overhauled.

McPhail stepped forward.

'Vassall,' he said decisively, repeating the newcomer's name. 'Father played for Repington in 1896. Was stated to be the best centre-forward the school ever had. Proved it by getting a bag of goals—five against Whitefriars. Afterwards walked into the Corinthians team, and played for England. The real judges say he was about the best known.'

Having thus rattled off his "piece," McPhail retired.

Stanhope stared hard.

'Vassall, of course!' he said, communing with himself. Bridges and Jenkins shifted forward in their chairs. The atmosphere became expectant.

'And do you play centre-forward, too?' inquired Stanhope. There was a new note in his voice. His tone was kindly, encouraging. With Stephenson gone, how badly we in Tads' wanted a first-rate centre-forward!'

'I am afraid I don't play football at all.'

A bombshell bursting could not have caused much more commotion. Stanhope fell back in his chair, his face quite ludicrous with surprise; Jenkins got off the side of the table; Bridges jumped as though someone had kicked him; and McPhail completed the havoc by letting the tea-pot slip out of his hands to be smashed to fragments on the floor.

I did what I could.

'You were delicate or something, weren't you, Vassall?' I asked.

The gratitude in the kid's eyes!

'Yes—but I'm not now. I'm fit now,' he replied, thus completely undoing all that I—very unwillingly, as you may imagine—had tried to do.

I could see Stanhope narrowing his eyes. This new kid had the look of breed about him—you remember I noticed his clean-cut appearance in the train: one would have said he was a football player at once. His very air of tenseness might have been mistaken for quivering eagerness when brought before the man who could put him in the house team.

'You're quite fit now, you say?' Stanhope's voice had become abrupt.

'Yes—quite.'

'Then, young-fellow-my-lad, you will play foot-ball whether you like it or not! We don't encourage slackers in Tads'. Haven't you heard that we used to be cock house at footer?'

'Yes—Watney told me.' He turned to me, but I am afraid I could give him no encouragement now. A Vassall, the son of Repington's proudest football product, the son of a man who had played not only for the Corinthians, but for England—and "he didn't play football at all." It was about the most awful moment I had known during my experience of Repington.

'That's all I have got to say. Only don't forget it. You will be warned when to turn out—but you will have to play, understand?'

'Yes.' He had gone white to his lips.

'Jumping snakes!' burst forth Stanhope, as Vassall, dismissed, had his hand on the door; 'if it's not too much to ask, why did you come to Repington, your guvnor's school, if you didn't think of playing football?'

The new boy made no reply.

This angered the Captain of Tads.'

'Is footer too rough for you? he barked; 'are you afraid of getting hurt?'

Again no reply—except that sudden, alarming pallor in the face.

'Clear out!' cried Stanhope, with infinite contempt. 'To think I should have lived to see the day when an able-bodied lout of fifteen stands in this room and tells me to my face that he doesn't play football! I say, Fireworks, if you have made a mistake and foisted off that thing that has just left the room as the son of Vassall who played for Corinth, when he's really the son of a wretched nonentity, you'll be for it!'

'That's rubbish, Stan' I put in; 'he's the son of Gilbert Vassall right enough—you can see the breed in him.'

'A pretty rotten breed,' snapped Bridges; 'why, he didn't say anything when you accused him of being a funk, Stanhope.'

'He didn't say anything—but did you notice how white he went?' This from McPhail, serious almost beyond recognition. 'That chap can play football, even if he's never touched a ball before in his life. I'm willing to swear to that. Hang it, there must be some-thing in heredity, or whatever they call the stuff! On the face of it that kid's the biggest failure as the son of a famous father that has ever existed—but there's something beneath the surface in this case, and I intend to poke about until I find out what it is.'

'Rot! the chap's a funk-shy!' snapped Stanhope, enraged, and the meeting broke up.

CHAPTER III

The Funk-shy

Tadburn's were out for footer practice, and the touch-lines were crowded.

The news had spread like a prairie-fire—how that the son of the Vassall whose name had been handed in reverence had come to Tads', and was playing in the house trial match that afternoon in the same position as his famous father—centre-forward. Those who wished us well, and those who wished us ill were there—the former to cheer, and the latter to weigh up and criticize.

There was quite a quiver of excitement in the crisp air. I felt it myself. Tads' had been cock house for so long, and now everyone—everyone except our most optimistic juniors—saw the once-famous house crumbling to pieces. Here was the very fabric of drama—a subject that some of the old Greeks might have woven into one of their pop-eye tragedies.

And the kid Vassall at centre-forward...

It was a grim jest on the part of Stanhope.

'I am inclined to agree with McPhail—although I admit I scoffed at the idea at first—that the kid has football in him; dash it, with such a father, he must have! What I intend to do is to knock that rotten funk out of him—that is why I have put him at centre-forward. Kill or cure, Dot-and-Carry, see? Either we make a player of him, or the shop will become too hot, and his people will be forced to take him away. A funk-shy in Tads—!'

I saw clearly enough.

'But if he has never really played before—' I fumbled, 'even though this is only a practice—you see what I mean, Stan?'

But Tads' Captain was a determined fellow.

'He's got to go through with it. Evans is on one side of him and Gill on the other. Both are goodish forwards. They have instructions to push the ball through to him. I had him in for an hour last night. I could get

10

precious little out of the fellow, but he did admit that he had *watched* plenty of footer, even if he had not played it. So that he knows the idea. Besides,' noticing my frown, I suppose, 'I had to try him *somewhere* in the game, Watney; he was the most likely-looking among all the new kids.'

This was certainly true, and I had no answer ready. Dash it, if a fellow came to Repington, he was naturally supposed to play football. As Jenkins once said: 'If a bloke doesn't come to the shop to play footer, what *does* he come here for?'

Although I knew Stanhope was right, although I knew that he would have the moral support of Tads', and the rest of the school behind him, yet I could not help feeling sorry for the boy he had pressed into what evidently was very unwilling service. But that anyone bearing the name of Vassall *should* be unwilling to play footer... Tads himself coming on to the field in sweater and shorts, I gave up speculating, and gave myself up to watching the game.

Before I write any more, I should explain that Repington is a soccer, and not a rugger, school. We had been one of the few big public schools who had remained true to the Corinthian code. Some rugger, and fairly good rugger, too, was played, but soccer was our chief sport. The ambition of every Rep when he left the shop was to play for Corinth— and a great many did. And now to get on.

The teams were lining up. I could see Vassall's white face. The fellow seemed to be unnerved: I swear he was trembling. Tads must have noticed, for he went across and spoke to him; asked him if he were unwell, I expect. Quite distinctly I saw Vassall shake his head. He remained on the field.

So far as the old house colours were concerned, the teams were fairly evenly matched. Thus the four best players—Stanhope, Jenkins, Bridges, and Birtles—were opposed; Stanhope and Jenkins (at centre-half right back respectively) on one side, and Bridges Birtles (at inside left and left back) on the other. The other two men who had played for the house the previous season were not brilliant, while the new stuff course was purely speculative.

'Something tells me, Watney, that we are on the eve of interesting events. Who was the bearded sage who said that the onlooker sees most of the game? Beshrew me, but I'm inclined to think he's right—one gets a better view from this elevation than if rooted beneath the goal posts.'

Needless to say—McPhail! The irrepressible would have been playing in goal for Stanhope's side that afternoon but for an injured shoulder.

'Watney,' he went on, 'I should like to have your views about this highly curious but interesting Vassall case before I apply my own deductive powers as Sheerluck Jones to the task. Although, at the present time, the youth is giving a highly realistic impersonation of an old-time Christian slave thrown to the famished lions, I still persist in believing that the fellow has some football in him. Ah!'

The whistle had gone, and Vassall had tapped the ball smartly to his inside right. The gesture had been that of one who knew his job. Surely the fellow had played before!

The inside right backheeled to Stanhope, and the skipper, side-stepping the onrushing opposing centre-forward, flung out wide to the right.

'A genius in the rough—name of Geekie!' I heard McPhail say, and then some one laughed. The next moment a veritable gale of mirth swept round the ground.

The outside right that Stanhope had commandeered was a striking-looking youth. To begin with, he was nearly six feet tall, and of an impressive lankiness. Indeed, he threatened to break off in half any moment. As for his legs, they were just sticks.

But Geekie—if that was his name—was plainly under the impression that he was a footballer. He sported a pair of bright yellow footer boots which were almost blinding to gaze upon; and, as the ball came out to him, he waved his left arm as much as to say: 'Now leave everything to me!'

'He got that from Meredith[1], the famous pro,' vouchsafed McPhail. 'This bird will be well worth watching. According to what I hear he can't help bringing home the bacon in Maths and all the other useless sciences —but what Geekie himself favours is his nifty work at outside right. We shall see.'

We soon saw: the lanky youth, with the huge spectacles, in an endeavour to trap the ball in an effectively spectacular manner—fell over it, and measured his long length on the grass!

'A bad start,' commented McPhail, as Bridges secured from the subsequent throw-in, and commenced one of his mesmeric dribbles. 'Oh, well played, sir!'

Stanhope, fretting at the chance which the angular Geekie had squandered, had gone in all-hearted to the tackle and had brought the brilliant Bridges up standing. The skipper, securing the ball, then dribbled a few feet, and swept forward a beautiful pass to Vassall.

'What did I tell you?' said McPhail in a fierce whisper.

---

[1] Billy Meredith was one of the first true footballing celebrities – even if not the best player of his generation, he was one of the most talked about. He was instrumental in the early rise to success of Manchester City, with whom he won an FA Cup, then crossed over to Manchester United where he went on to win 2 league titles and a further FA Cup.

Vassall had instantly got the ball under control. A cheer came from the touch-lines. The ability to play footer can be seen unmistakably in one flick of the boot. Vassall the boy who had stated that he did not play football, had shown this talent. The reason was not understandable, but I felt distinctly bucked. From the start I had been anxious that he should make good.

Then, in common with the rest of the watchers, I had to gasp. Although he had snapped up the skipper's pass so neatly, now that he had the ball at his feet, and had a comparatively clear course in front of him, Vassall seemed smitten with fright.

'Go on, man!' shouted Stanhope, rushing up.

'Dribble!' roared the touch-lines; 'dribble, you fool!'

But Vassall remained still. And worse was to come. When Sayers, the opposing left half, came rushing up, Vassall surrendered the ball to him with scarcely any attempt at a struggle. The fellow seemed stricken.

That sort of thing isn't tolerated at Repington. But, for that matter, it was practically unprecedented, even amongst new kids. And this boy was much taller and stronger-looking altogether than Sayers whom he had allowed to rob him of the ball, practically without a tussle at all.

'Funk! Rotten funk!' came the scathing cries of criticism.

Just then the ball went outside, and the whole crowd of us saw an infuriated Stanhope rush up to Vassall, and roar something at him. I could guess what it was. The most unholy thing on earth to the skipper was a funk-shy.

It would be charitable to draw a veil over the rest of the match. Such a spectacle had never been seen in a Tads' House match within my recollection. It may have been "nerves" instead of pure, unadulterated funk, but Vassall gave the most disgraceful exhibition that could be imagined. An opponent had only to show up for him to draw back in obvious terror. It wasn't the chances he missed, it was the display of wretched poltroonery that was so sickening. The fellow showed himself a rank coward. Eventually Stanhope, after talking with Tads, told him to leave the field. That was after he had literally swerved aside—leaving the ball—when Birtles, who I admit was a heavy tackler at the best of times, came charging at him, and bowled him over heavily.

It was horrible. His face as white as a sheet, and his head hung low, Vassall left the field amid the concentrated groans of every junior watching the game. The seniors had better manners, and were more disciplined, but on every face was open or covert contempt. And to think that it was a Tads' fellow!

Stanhope's team lost by three goals to one, but who cared about the result? That was the merest incidental: the only thing that counted, of course, was the slur that had been cast upon the house. Within five minutes the whole place would be shrieking and reeking with it.

I hobbled up to Stanhope when the teams left the pitch. But he wasn't able to speak just then.

We walked across the field, and then the skipper said, 'Come in and see me at tea, old man.'

As was to be supposed, Tads' could talk of nothing else: I found the house almost standing on its head with wrath. Small groups of indignant protesters were everywhere—there was some talk about lugging the funk-shy out and ducking him in the river which meandered its placid way past the bottom of Big Field.

I scotched that, although I had many black looks. But it was known that Stanhope himself had said that the rotter should be chucked out of the house, and once that rumour gained full currency it was impossible to check the tumult.

Vassall, it seemed, had gone straight to his study, and had barricaded himself in. Directly this information was brought by an inquisitive junior a general move was made towards the corridor. There ensued a tremendous hammering on the study door, and a cry: 'Come out, funk! Come and show yourself!'

I would have tried to stop it had I thought it would have been any good. But I moved nearer to see that no great mischief was done. With feeling running so high—for Tads' was very jealous of its sporting honour —Vassall might easily get a very rough time.

'Come and show yourself!—funk!'

The cries rose higher, shriller, and had more menace in them. Tads' was determined not to be frustrated of its revenge.

Then a most amazing thing happened quite suddenly: the door of the study opened, and in the opening was—Vassall! His face was pale, but he looked straight at his accusers. There was no flinching. Even granted that he must have called upon his last moral resources, his action, coming straight after the ignominy of the football field, was startling.

'What do you want?' I heard him ask.

The question was so unexpected that it staggered the crowd of persecutors. 'What did they want?' The colossal cheek of the fellow! 'What did they want?' They would jolly soon show him what they wanted!

'We want to tell you that we don't have funks in Tads'!' shrilled a junior, and, although it was only young Bessell who had said it, a chorus of approving yells went up. And whilst these cries were filling the corridor with sound, Birtles, having changed, came in.

In the ordinary school story, I suppose, Birtles would be cast for the villain of the piece, the house bully. He was neither of these things, but

14

for all that he was a rather unpleasant person to have about the place. His one redeeming feature was his football; beyond that he was neither ornamental nor useful. He went through life with a sneer, and when he wasn't sneering, he scowled. He was thick set, and, although only the age of Vassall, or perhaps a little older, report had it that he shaved. He had a supreme contempt for practically everyone else in the house, except Stanhope. He never worked, and openly scorned anyone who did. That was Birtles.

He took in the situation quickly. An unpleasant smile appeared on his dark face. Striding through the staring crowd, he planted himself in front of Vassall.

'Well, my brave hero!' he said, this starting a general titter, of course; 'what do you mean by showing yourself to the public gaze twice in one day?' His tone suddenly sharpened. 'What right has a fellow like you to come here, in any case? You rotten, white-livered funk!—I have a good mind to start punching some guts into you straightaway!'

Then the bombshell came.

'Start, then, Birtles!' Vassall had spoken in a level voice.

Can you picture the scene: the fellow who had the contempt of the whole school not an hour previously now looking straight into the face of the would-be avenger of his house's honour?

'Land him one, Birtles!' 'Take the cheek out of Birtles!'

I confess I made no attempt to interrupt. Much as I was against him, my interest in this astonishing newcomer had not abated; on the other hand, it had increased. And if I had interrupted, the charge against Vassall would have been strengthened: it would have been said that he got me to stop Birtles from punching him. That would not have been true, of course, but, like many other untruths, it would have sufficed.

'Do you think that chap really *is* a funk, Watney?'

McPhail, just arrived, caught hold of my arm, and squeezed it. His tone was one of incredulity. Vassall was still standing openly facing Birtles. He had not raised his hands, but I noticed that his fists were clenched.

'Land into him, Birtles!' The juniors were eager for the sight of blood. And this unexpected confounding of their general belief had not only surprised but annoyed them.

Birtles sneered—and then turned away. Perhaps he hadn't the conscience to do it—to hit a fellow who had already proved himself such a cowardly worm; perhaps the thought that the scrap would be too hopelessly one-sided did not give him the necessary zest; perhaps—although this, no doubt, was an absurd theory—the straight look that the proved funk gave him—no, it could not have been that. But, anyway,

15

Birtles turned away: with a sneer, of course—he wouldn't have been Birtles if he hadn't sneered.

'You precious mamma's boy!' he jeered. 'He's not worth punching,' he added in explanation of his strange abstinence.

A vivid flush dyed Vassall's face. He made a step forward.

'If you fellows will only be decent enough to listen,' he said in a low voice which those on the outskirts of the crowd could barely catch, 'I want to say that I'm sorry for—for this afternoon.'

During the deep silence of amazement that followed, Vassall turned, and the study door shut after him.

CHAPTER IV

In Which Another Strange Thing Happens

Peter McPhail had a big heart as well as an abnormal brain. By nature he was always on the side of smaller nations; all lowly creatures he endeavoured to succour, which meant that for the aristocratic bosses of this world he had a hotly-burning rage. Especially did he dislike Birtles. He disliked him on sight, on principle, and on every other reasonable and unreasonable ground.

As courageous himself as any red-headed youngster expected to be, McPhail in the ordinary way would have been the first to condemn anyone who had openly shown himself to be a funk. McPhail professed a good deal of contempt for many of the traditions of Repington, but in his loyal regard for his house, he yielded none. Tads' was all that it should be, in his eyes. Nothing too much could be done for it; no sacrifice too great, no effort too tremendous. On the face of things he should have hardened his heart against the coward who had disgraced the house in the eyes of the whole school.

But—as he explained to me subsequently—he simply could not do it with regard to Vassall. There was something about the chap which drew you to him. The fellow had a tragic air: he seemed more the plaything thing of Fate, the sport of Destiny, than the poor weakling which his conduct on the footer field would have led one to believe. There was a thoughtful strain in McPhail's character in striking contrast to the wild foolhardiness he showed at times: he saw beneath the surface of things. Always intrigued by an interesting problem, he determined that Vassall presented a puzzle which it would be worth his while to try to solve. This, and the fact that he had liked Vassall on sight, caused him to stand by the funk-shy when all the rest of the house were against him.

Vassall, as it happened, was in the same dormitory —the seventh. After suffering persecution during the whole of prep the house outcast had further trials to undergo when he got to bed that night.

Directly lights were out, conversation became general, except on the part of Vassall and McPhail. There was no hesitation about the choice of subject. One topic was in everyone's mouth.

'Rotten funk! He ought to be kicked out!' Then some hissing—a lot of hissing.

McPhail got out of bed. Hill, the prefect in charge of the seventh, was a wonky reed. He saw McPhail, but felt that silence was the better part of discretion.

McPhail walked across to Vassall's bed.

'These fools will soon get tired; in the meantime, don't take any notice,' he said, and walked back again.

'I say, Hill,' he remarked on the return journey, 'what about a little healthful slumber, eh? Or perhaps you wouldn't mind me shying a few slippers at the yappers?'

'Stop that talking there!' called Hill, in his best imitation of a prefect's roar.

The talking continued.

'Shut up!' yelled McPhail, and hurled slipper No.1.

There was a startled cry—and then silence.

McPhail essentially had a way with him.

Repington overlooked a small town. Fact being stranger than fiction, there actually was a constant feud raging between the "Bloods" of the school and those benighted denizens of the town whom McPhail, in his terse fashion, styled the "louts of the village." The latter consisted in the main of hobble-de-hoys who spent the bigger portion of their existence lounging on the pavements, making highly offensive remarks to some of the passers-by, and certain errand boys. Included in the latter group was Nobby Durrance, who acted as winged messenger for Mr. Chandler, leading purveyor of the town.

On the principle that he did not add to the decorative beauty of life, McPhail had exchanged a few unpleasantries with Nobby. Let it be said, to avoid any possible misunderstanding, that Nobby had started the batting. One day as he was hurtling through space, standing up in his bicycle stirrups, urging his burden along, he had reached out a grimy hand and snatched McPhail's school cap from off the red head. (School caps were valuable trophies to the louts of the village.)

Now, McPhail was the last person in the world to suffer without rebuke such an indignity. To begin with, there was a new cap to be purchased—this in itself, a week from the end of the month, was no small matter—and, more important than the financial side, was the stain to the soul. McPhail commenced to think out a scheme of reprisal.

18

Thus it happened that one day not long after the initial skirmish, McPhail, passing Nobby as he rode his way with the meat-basket heavily laden, thoughtfully sprinkled both Nobby and his meat with some choicely prepared tincture of sulphuretted hydrogen. Sulphuretted hydrogen, without doubt, is one of the most potent perfumes that science has yet perfected—and McPhail had seen to it that what he carried was an especially fragrant brew. The result, we may safely presume, was lamentable; there were distressing scenes at each business call Nobby made that day.

Time had not lessened Nobby's hurt; he had waited patiently. All through the long summer holidays, he had nursed his wrath. He even ticked off the days on a calendar.

As for McPhail, the matter had almost slipped from his mind. He had dealt with Nobby, solving his knotty problem as he had been forced to solve others, and there, to all intents and purposes, the matter had ended. He did not visualize the fact that Nobby's narrow and restricted mind had concentrated on the matter to the exclusion of everything else.

Behold, then, the vengeful Nobby suddenly pouncing upon his prospective victim, as McPhail passed an alley-way not far from Mr. Chandler's excellent purveying business.

'Got yer!' exclaimed Nobby, in boastful triumph, and launched a terrific right swing.

McPhail was small, but he was wiry. Moreover, as the reader by this time has probably judged, he carried his wits always about with him.

It did not take him long to sum up the present position. One consequence of this was that he was able to avoid the worst consequences of that vicious right swing of Nobby's, although the half-blow that landed jarred him considerably. Another result was that McPhail realized it was plainly a question of either Nobby or himself, and he did not intend it to be himself.

All was going well for Repington—although McPhail was considerably outweighted—when a cohort of village louts, sworn pals of Nobby's, hove in sight round the nearest corner. Seeing a Repington school cap they hastened.

Suddenly McPhail felt himself in the midst of a scrimmage which was rapidly bearing him down. He strove desperately and furiously, but someone hacked at his shins with what appeared to be clogs, and he fell to the pavement.

It was then that a counter avalanche occurred. Whilst he was still on the ground, struggling hard to get free of the turmoil, a youth wearing a school cap plunged into the midst of the fray, hitting out to right and left with Trojan-like blows. Nobby himself received a juicy left that did his

19

squat nose considerable harm, and his associates' groans were testimony that the newcomer was as impartial as he was effective. It was not long before a passing policeman applied the closure, Nobby and his army taking advantage by retreating for cover.

'I say, are you hurt?'

McPhail was dragged to his feet. He took one look at his rescuer, and then rubbed his eyes. For a moment he thought he must be dreaming.

'*Vassall!*' he said.

It was the footer funk-shy! He hadn't a mark on him, but he looked very confused.

'Look here, is there any place where we can get some coffee?' he asked, 'because if so, will you come and have a chat with me? I rather want to, you know, if you don't mind.'

For once in his life, McPhail found not a word to say. Instead, he did the practical thing. He led the way to Lake's.

After the second coffee, McPhail allowed himself to speak.

'Well, I'm dashed!' he said, and then, reddening with confusion, added: 'I'm jolly grateful to you, Vassall! I was down, and likely to have been out, if you hadn't pitched in. It was purely an affair between myself and a friend of mine called Nobby—but several of Nobby's pals butted in like the sportsmen they are, just before you arrived. My word, you let 'em have it properly!' He looked keenly at his rescuer. 'Ever done any boxing?'

'No-o.' Vassall seemed confused.

'Then you ought to take it up. There's only this chap Dempsey who seems any good at it nowadays, and there's bags of coin in it.'

Vassall was thoughtful.

'I don't know you very well,' he said, 'but you have been so decent that—that I would like to ask you a favour.'

'Anything you like!' promptly answered the other.

'Will you keep this to yourself? Don't say anything about it back at the school, I mean?'

'Why?' sharply.

'Because I wish you wouldn't—that's all. I don't say that people wouldn't believe you, but— In any case, it's nothing to talk about. You would have done the same for me.'

'Certainly I would, but there's a difference all the same. Vassall, do you mind if I speak rather plainly?—I'm a pal of yours from now on—if you're agreeable,' McPhail added in explanation.

'No—I don't mind. I think I know what you are going to say.'

'Well, then, I'll say it. You waded in like a hero just now, but at footer, the other day—'

Vassall nodded. He did not seem to bear any resentment.

'I can't tell you, McPhail. I oughtn't to have turned out.'

'But you can play footer, man! Directly you touched the ball you proved it! I had said so before—told Watney, that lame prefect. I say, do you mind if I tell Watney? He's a decent chap, and will keep it under his hat. He likes you, or I wouldn't ask.'

'Likes me?' Vassall's tone was incredulous and bitter; 'I fancied everyone in the house hated me—as they have every right to do, of course.'

McPhail slapped his hand on the table.

'Some more cakes,' he told the hurrying waitress, and to Vassall: 'I won't tell a soul beyond Watney, but I've got a scheme, Vassall; will you listen to it?'

CHAPTER V

Preparation

'Yes, of course I will listen,' replied Vassall. Something about McPhail had touched his imagination. He leaned across the table.

McPhail finished a cake.

'Jolly good currants,' he commented appreciatively, wetting a forefinger, and by this means picking up what crumbs remained on his plate. 'Well, my idea is this: you ought to make a fairly useful boxer if you took it up seriously: that left of yours is particularly juicy when you get it in. Now I could put you on to a man—'

'Who would teach me boxing?'

'Who would turn you out quite a respectable reliable article,' answered McPhail. 'You might find it an advantage to be able to use your dukes a bit, you know.'

Vassall flushed. A light suddenly came into his eyes.

'I say, can you take me to this chap now? Who is he?'

'His name's Benny Bennison. He's an old prize-ring scrapper, a regular dyed-in-the-wool bruiser—but the kindest hearted cove you could wish to meet. He wouldn't hurt a fly—but you've got to watch out for those half-arm jolts of his. I've seen him knock a chap nearly through the wall, and his fist hadn't travelled more than a few inches.'

McPhail keenly watched the effect of the last few words, but the gleam in the other's eyes didn't die down. Instead—'

'I say, does he do any real fighting now?—in the ring, I mean,' said Vassall.

'No—he's too old. But he trains a lot of likely lads.' McPhail's tone was very professional.

Benny Bennison proved to be a short, stocky man with humorous eyes that relieved the striking ugliness of his face. He reminded Vassall at once of a battered bulldog.

'On my right Benny Bennison, Middle-weight Champion of England, 1910-14; on my left David Vassall, aspirant after fistic honours,' announced McPhail impressively.

Vassall looked at the ex-pugilist with obvious admiration.

'It's jolly fine to be a champion, isn't it?'

Benny Bennison grinned—likeably. 'Well, I'm not denyin' that I was a very proud man when they handed me the Wronsbury Belt after beatin' Parky McFarlane at the National, sir.'

'Now, Benny, we're here to talk business,' cut in McPhail briskly; 'we can hold a reminiscence class another day. What we want to know is: how soon can you start Vassall here on his upward path? In other words, when can you commence giving him lessons?'

'As soon as ever the young gentleman likes,' was the equally prompt reply. 'If he's anxious to get on, he can't start too early.'

'I'm anxious all right,' said Vassall. Plainly he was determined.

'Well now, I'm willing to make my time suit yours, sir.'

'After tea strikes me as being by far the best arrangement—starting to-morrow,' said McPhail, and so it was arranged.

'Perhaps you'd like to see the gym, sir, if you have time to spare?' suggested Bennison; 'it won't be any novelty to Mr. McPhail, because he's been here before—'

'Amongst my many other ambitions,' supplemented McPhail turning to Vassall, 'is to find a likely lad that I can back to win the Middleweight Crown for England.'

'This way, sir.' The ex-pugilist was evidently used to the eccentricities of speech of the red-headed youth, for he made no comment, but led the party forward.

At the end of the garden-path was a huge shed which the former boxing champion had turned into a thoroughly up-to-date gymnasium. Here were found all the impedimenta of Bennison's manly trade—punch-balls, physical exercisers, dumb-bells, a medicine-ball, skipping ropes—there was even a shower-bath in a screened-off corner.

Vassall at once started on an interested tour of inspection. Bennison came over to McPhail.

'He looks a likely lad, sir,' he said, 'and there's no doubt he's keen.'

'Look here, Benny,' said the red-headed boy with such earnestness that the boxing-instructor stared. 'I want you to work over this chap as though your life depended upon it! If it's a question of extra money—'

'He's a friend of yours, Mr. McPhail, and extra money won't enter into it. Besides, I like the look of the young gentleman. make him just as good as he can be made.'

McPhail, as he walked back to Tads' with his protégé, smiled as though conscious of having made a good start with a worthy work. Schemes which had a sporting chance of coming off were a speciality of his.

Vassall himself was quiet. He had a lot to think about.

In the meantime, back at the school, something was brewing. Birtles was the brewer. It was certainly not want of physical courage which had caused him to treat contemptuously the challenge that Vassall, the funk-shy, had made to him after the footer trial match. Birtles was somewhat slow in grasping things, and, moreover, he was so astonished at what the other had said that he was late in realizing the real significance of the words.

Although not the quickest of thinkers, as has been intimated, he realized that his reputation had received something of a set-back, and, however much he may have professed not to trouble about what other people thought, Birtles was abnormally sensitive on the point. He liked to feel that directly he scowled most of his immediate world trembled. Before that lapse of his the juniors in the house had fled to corners directly he raised his voice. Now they threatened to smile as he passed them. That was bad. He would have to remedy it.

On this particular afternoon, Birtles, after much cogitation, had his brain-wave. Being slow-witted, it followed almost as a natural consequence that he was seldom original in his ideas.

It was the mental slur that hurt Birtles. He was so confident of being able to beat the funk-shy in a stand-up scrap that, in a feeling of groping sportsmanship, he fought down the inclination to batter Vassall's head for him. He wanted to humiliate the fellow in some other way.

That was why—not being very bright—he decided upon ragging Vassall's study. No better plan occurred to him.

In a lordly, off-hand way he communicated the bare outline of the scheme to three other fellows, slightly unbending in doing so.

The suggestion was received with tremendous enthusiasm. All three auxiliaries were anxious to sun themselves in Birtles' good graces.

'I say, Birtles,' said Overton, 'let's do the thing properly, wear masks, eh?'

'Masks! You ass!' replied the leader, 'what do you want to wear masks for? You aren't afraid to let the fellow see you, are you?'

'Of course not!' answered Overton, his tone too emphatic to be natural, 'but it would give a little spice to it, you see.

Birtles was still contemptuous, but he relaxed so far as to ask growlingly where the masks were coming from.

'As it happens, I've got some in my trunk. We used them at Christmas—at a rag we had at home. Shall I get them?'

Birtles, still growling most ungraciously, intimated that he might.

Half an hour after he had returned from the town. Vassall was sitting alone, quietly reading, when the door opened noiselessly. Before he had time to get out of his chair, none too gentle hands had gripped him.

'What's the matter?' he started, but he could no further, for a football-stocking pushed into his mouth proved a very effective gag. The cries that he might have made would have been drowned in its deep woolliness. That is, if he had made them. He preferred not to, but saved his breath in the endeavour to put up as strong a struggle as possible against unequal odds.

It did not last very long. It would have been against the natural order of things had it done so, because there were five—Merridew had begged as a special favour to join the raiding party at the last moment—intrepid spirits in black masks, and they went to work with a merry will.

They literally left no stone unturned. In other words, they made a rare mess of the study. Ink flowed like water when the tap has been left running. Books came tumbling out of a bookcase which toppled majestically and crashingly to the floor. A heavy boot went clean through a basket-chair.

This was after the tenant had been rendered powerless: bound effectively hand and foot with stout rope, Vassall had been placed in the alcove lately occupied by the dismantled bookcase, and there he heard everything but saw nothing—for a tired-looking handkerchief—Merridew's—had been placed over his eyes, and the ends knotted at the back of his head. The job had been thoroughly done.

Eventually the room looked as though a gang of disappointed burglars had been through it. No effort was spared.

Only one more duty remained. The most burly of the marauders wrote large letters on a white card and pinned it to the coat of the victim.

Tads, otherwise Edward Timothy Stanley Tadburn, house-master, was passing along a corridor when he saw through the open door of a particular study such a state of confusion and chaotic disorder as, with all his experience, he had not set eyes upon for many years.

In duty bound he looked in. His initial start of surprise was repeated —only considerably magnified. He saw a boy blindfolded, and with ankles and wrists secured, standing in a corner, and bearing upon his breast a card on which was crudely printed in huge letters the words—

I AM A FUNK.

Tads was not a man to waste time in useless words. He strode over to the captive and quickly released him.

'What's the meaning of this, Vassall?'

The released prisoner blinked.

'I scarcely know, sir—for certain,' he said.

'You know who did it?'

'I couldn't see, sir—they tied this bandage round my eyes.'

'H'm!' Tads liked that in the boy. Vassall knew, of course—he must have known.

'Well, I'll see that this sort of thing does not occur again. In the meantime,'—pointing to the card of ignominy— 'you had better destroy that.'

'I intend to keep it, sir!' replied Vassall.

Tads wisely did not ask the reason. Perhaps he had a guess at the truth. Appearances were against this boy with the famous name, but—

It took Vassall a long time to repair the damage, but according to McPhail, who gave him valuable assistance, he did not seem to mind.

The card he locked carefully away in a cupboard.

CHAPTER VI

"Gated"

'As a matter of solid fact,' said McPhail, 'you're a liar! Also, you're a somewhat sketchy washer. If you weren't, I'd lay violent hands upon you.'

'Think yourself clever, don't you?' snapped Greenslade.

'My boy, what I really think—especially about you—would send you into convulsions. Leave me, varlet!'

I hobbled up in time to hear the parting phrases of what had evidently been a heated argument.

'What's the storm about!' I asked McPhail as Greenslade, a particularly obnoxious junior, faded away.

McPhail became more serious than I had ever known him.

'It's those yarns about Vassall. That unwashed earwig started to jaw about Vassall splitting to Tads over having his study ragged. I told him he was a liar, and that, if he wasn't such a mouldy blighter, I'd have clipped him one across the jaw. Watney,' very earnestly, 'I wasn't there when Tads came in, but I'm pretty sure that Vassall didn't split. He's going to settle with Birtles another way.'

'How?' for McPhail had turned very mysterious all of a sudden.

'I'll tell you later on,' he replied, 'but, in the meantime, you can take it from me that Vassall isn't *all* wrong—there's a fair lot of good in the chap.' He paused, to go on more quickly: 'You've heard me speak of the illustrious Nobby, haven't you?'

I nodded. Nobby's name loomed large in contemporary Repington records.

'Well,' resumed McPhail, 'I'm going to tell you something startling. But you must promise to keep it absolutely to yourself. Going down town the other afternoon, I was suddenly set upon by the fair Nobby. That was all right: the blighter biffed me in the stomach to begin with, and that got my blood up. What really mattered was that several of Nobby's stalwart pals shot round the corner. It was a case of about six or seven to one

27

when up crops a fellow wearing the school cap! He set about the rotters in splendid style, displaying a really juicy left to particular advantage. What was more, he lugged two of the worms off my chest and got me to my feet. Now tell me, most grave and reverend Master Watney, who was that selfsame Repington scholar?'

'Not—not Vassall?'

'Vassall, and none other! Retain in your memory my words about a particularly juicy left, because the time will come when they will flash inevitably to your mind like a message from home. Adios!' Making a salutation, which he no doubt fondly imagined was Spanish, McPhail wandered off.

This was startling news with a vengeance—the funk-shy turned heroic rescuer! My feelings towards Vassall have already been shown, and but for the promise which McPhail had exacted from me, I should have liked nothing better than to spread the news all over the school.

What had McPhail up his sleeve? What was the meaning of his smile, and the insistence with which he drove home the astonishing facts that Vassall, the funk-shy, first of all had a "particularly juicy left", and secondly, that he knew how to use it? I wish I had known—and yet on second thoughts I decided that the dramatic development (and with McPhail mixed up in the matter there was sure to be a dramatic development) would come with all the more welcome *éclat* if it was totally unexpected.

Dramatic developments seemed to be in the air just about then. Into Big Hall, the Reverend Joseph Mildmay, Head of Repington, strode that night, and, from the commanding altitude of his big desk, made a fevered announcement.

'In spite of repeated warnings,' he thundered, in his memorable deep voice, 'boys of this school have again become embroiled with certain individuals of the town. Yesterday afternoon, I am informed, there was a most regrettable and disgraceful scene witnessed at the corner of the High Street... As a consequence, the town will be declared out of bounds — from to-morrow until further notice!'

Fellows stared at the Head, but he did not vouchsafe any further information. Like the unchallengeable autocrat that he was, he had hurled forth his fiat and then departed, leaving a state of the wildest confusion behind. The whole school, seniors as well as juniors, to be kept from the town!

As the school was breaking up into little sections, McPhail caught the arm of the Repington Ishmael.

'I say, Vassall, I shall have to let it out now—you see that, don't you?

28

We can't let the whole shop suffer. You don't mind?'

'You mustn't say that I was in it!' replied the other swiftly; 'say that you were helped by—by an outsider.'

'All right,' agreed McPhail, with a queer smile, 'I will! I'm going straight off to Stanhope now. He will see Tads, and Tads will see the Head. I'll bet you that the town will be open to all after the Head's heard the yarn.'

But no pronouncement was made to that effect by half-past four on the following afternoon. The veto on the town was still in existence.

This fact worried Vassall. He was in a dilemma. He either had to run the risk of incurring a severe punishment, or he had to miss the appointment he had made with Benny Bennison to receive his first boxing lesson. It was time he was off. In another minute or so McPhail would probably be back from another talk with Stanhope. He didn't want to see McPhail. If he saw McPhail he knew what would happen—the red-headed boy would accompany him on his adventurous trip. That would mean that McPhail would stand the chance of being caught as well as himself.

The thought of not keeping the appointment with Bennison was like an acid eating into his blood. A fierce determination was driving him— had driven him, in fact, ever since McPhail had taken him to see the old Middle-weight Champion the day before.

Another few seconds, and Vassall had made up his mind—quite definitely made up his mind.

In the far corner of the playing-field a large tree effectively shielded anyone who wished to climb the steep wall. Vassall, five minutes after coming to his resolution, dropped from this wall into a manure bed belonging to a nursery-gardener. He was not seen, and the next minute he was speeding to that part of the town which housed Benny Bennison's Select and Up-to-date Gymnasium.

The ex-champion was unfeignedly pleased to see him. Bennison's welcoming smile did much to compensate Vassall for the thought of what would happen to him if he were discovered.

And, for the next half-hour, he had no time for extraneous thought of any description. He was too busy listening to what the ex-champion was telling him, and doing his best to follow out the instructions he received. At the end of that half-hour he decided that he knew nothing whatever about boxing—and that he would never know: he was too hopeless a fool!

He was surprised, therefore, to hear his instructor exclaim: 'An' not at all bad, sir, for a first try-out! That left of yours is goin' to be useful afore you've finished. The straight left was what won me the championship, so I ought to know. A very nice left you'll have when you get on a bit, Mr. Vassall. The same time to-morrow, sir?'

'Yes,' replied Vassall.

The thing now was to get back safely. But the gods were against him. Just as he was taking the turn in Stapleford Hill he saw Tads. What was more important, Tads saw him.

'You realize what you have done, I suppose, Vassall?'

'Yes, sir.'

'Have you any reasonable explanation to give me?'

Vassall did not hesitate.

'I have no explanation, sir.'

Tads frowned.

'I like confidence, Vassall,' he said sternly. 'However, get back.'

When Vassall returned to Repington via the high wall at the back of the playing-field, he learned that the Head had removed the ban on the town!

For a moment Vassall thought of going to the master and telling Tads the reason of his breaking bounds. Then he decided against the resolution.

In the end Tads sent for him.

'You will be "gated" for three days, Vassall. If you had only been open, and told me— I dislike fellows who refuse to give me their confidence. Have you anything to say?'

'No, sir,' replied Vassall. He had his code, and if he spoke now this code would be broken. This explanation, like other things, he felt could wait.

CHAPTER VII

McPhail Takes Over

During the week that Vassall was 'gated', Tads' played Dormer's in the first inter-house match of the season. After a desperate struggle they lost 2–1. Twenty minutes before the end they were two goals down, and had not scored themselves. Then Stanhope, desperate, shifted Bridges from inside-left to centre-forward, and 'Bumper' rushed the ball through from a corner.

'It's a centre-forward we want, sir—as you can see for yourself, of course,' Stanhope said to Tads after the match. 'Bridges is a fine inside man, but if I move him to centre, the left wing goes phut.'

'I quite agree. Besides, Bridges, although he scored to-day, is not a centre-forward... Well, we must do the best we can, Stanhope. Someone will turn up, perhaps.'

'Jolly vague and unsatisfactory that,' muttered the captain to Bridges and Jenkins when he returned to his study. 'We've gone through the place with a fine-toothed comb for a centre-forward—and he simply doesn't exist! I wouldn't have minded if it had been Canaver's that had licked us to-day: Canaver's are the strongest house on paper in the shop this year. But Dormer's!' The speaker waved hands despairingly.

'There wasn't much wrong with the defence, Stan,' said Jenkins. 'Those two goals they got were fine shots—we must admit that; it was because our forwards couldn't get going—oh, you were all right, Bridges, but Hastings in the centre and Towlinson at outside-right were punk! Ah! well—' Yawning, he went out.

The defeat on the football field had its influence upon the house for the rest of the day. After you have been cock house at any sport, it seems a trifle hard to take a licking from a house you had formerly more or less despised. The year before Tads' would have walked through Dormer's crowd.

That night before prep McPhail sought out the house Ishmael. 'Hurry up with your boxing, Vassall,' he said, 'because I have another proposition to put before you.'

As usual Vassall displayed eagerness.

'What is it?' he inquired.

'I won't worry you with details now,' McPhail replied provokingly, 'but you have heard the news, I suppose: that the house lost to Dormer's to-day, because they hadn't either a centre-forward or an outside-right?'

Before Vassall could make any comment he was gone.

'I say, Mac, what's the idea?'

Even Vassall smiled—and David Vassall had had very little at which to smile since the defeat of Tads' by Dormer's. This football catastrophe —it was regarded as nothing less by everyone in Tads'—had accentuated his position as house Ishmael. 'A centre-forward—a centre-forward! That's what the team wants,' everyone said. And then almost everyone remembered that there was a chap named Vassall in the house—a fellow whose father had been one of the finest centres who had ever lived, but who had funked so badly on the field himself that the team captain had refused to play him again!

Of course it was rough on Hastings, the fellow who had played—or had tried to play—centre against Dormer's, but it was much rougher on Vassall. However, he was away from the shop now—a good two miles away—and he smiled. The reason of his quiet mirth was—Geekie. Brief mention has been made before in these pages of a youth named Geekie— George Gregory Geekie, to give him his full title.

G. G. Geekie was attached to Tads'. Attached is the word I have chosen after due deliberation. Geekie was not only a member of the house, but he loved Tads' with a very great love. He yearned to do something for it, something heroic—something with a possibility of death in it.

A curious case, Geekie's—not uncommon, may be, but singular all the same. Perhaps the brainiest fellow in the whole school, certainly in his own house, he professed an utter contempt for all branches of learning and devoted practically all his time to a serious study of athletics. That he was invariably top of his form was not so much an honour in Geekie's eyes as a misfortune.

Geekie's father was perhaps at the back of the whole thing. A professor of economics at a northern university, he had passed on abnormal brain-power to his son as another parent passes on a Roman nose or a weakness in the stomach. But Geekie hated brain: I he worshipped only brawn, and the feats which brawn can do in athletics.

We all have our weaknesses, our pet desires—Geekie's was no stranger, perhaps, than many others: he merely wished to play outside-right for Repington! At the time the footer season had opened he had

32

about as much chance of achieving this laudable ambition as he had of entering Parliament as a Cabinet Minister. But, nothing daunted, George Gregory Geekie dreamed his dreams.

The unfortunate thing so far was that no one had been induced to take him seriously. Stanhope had grinned, Jenkins had howled, Bridges had slapped him on the back and said that he was the funniest chap he'd ever struck. Afterwards the three had talked about Geekie's spider-like legs, and his gig-lamps which, being badly-fitted, slipped up and down the would-be winger's nose like a boy on roller-skates.

The Big Three had reason enough for their scepticism, they thought. Anyone less unlike an outside-right never appeared to offer himself as a candidate for football honours. Geekie looked like a boy in hard training as a cerebral-wizard—a fellow who lived on raw nuts, and who spent what time he could spare from translating Virgil into Sanskrit in chasing the Fourth Dimension round the Solar System into the inner lairs of bimetallism. Nothing like an outside-right, really!

But McPhail had been in Stanhope's study when Geekie came to offer himself, and it was McPhail who had pointed out to the House Football Captain what latent possibilities there might be in Geekie's abnormally long legs. Stanhope had roared, but, as a concession to his favoured fag, had included Geekie in the trial match.

Who could hope to portray the feelings which Geekie had on that historic afternoon? After being word-perfect in the *Life of William Meredith*, after having studied all the diagrams and photographs, after reading every line that had been printed about the Art of Wing Play during the past ten years, he was actually on the field of play himself. There was no doubt about it: the wind made his football knickers flap, he felt the keen air cold about his bare knees, the new footer boots, which he had soaked liberally in boiling water to make them supple and yielding to the feet—("Hints on Boots" by A Famous International, *Splodder's Weekly*)—showed up a vivid yellow against the green turf. Yes, Geekie was there, and seemingly well equipped.

Alas! that the fulfilment did not come up to the promise of the resplendent gear. Geekie did not do a single thing like his immortal hero, William Meredith, except wave his left hand towards the goal mouth. Apart from that there was no resemblance; comparison simply ended. Where Meredith would have dribbled with masterly precision, Geekie stumbled; where Meredith would have centred in immaculate fashion, aiming for the juncture of far upright and cross-bar, Geekie spurned the ball outside. Geekie, if the brutal truth must be told, was more of a figure of mirth than of plaudits.

Yet standing on the touch-line was at least one person who saw deeper than the ludicrous stumbles and the foolish prances.

'He can run,' McPhail had said to himself, 'even if he runs without the ball. I shall have to make him run *with* the ball.'

In pursuance of this worthy aim, McPhail now put the deflated football (which he had produced like a conjuror from an overcoat pocket) between his knees, inserted the end of a bicycle pump in the nose of the bladder and commenced to fill the latter with air at an alarming pace. Five minutes later a ball, gloriously hard, bounced upon the grass.

Like a general addressing troops, McPhail said a few words.

'You chaps must forgive the innocent deception,' he remarked; 'I said a walk—well, we have had our walk. Now we're going to get in some footer practice.'

While the others stared, he proceeded: 'Before I've finished with you two, Vassall will be playing centre-forward for the house, and perhaps for the shop, and you, Geekie, will be outside-right for the house—there's so much hard work to be put in over you that I can't promise any more than that in your case.'

It was then that Vassall had smiled once more. It was not a satirical smile; on the contrary, it was a smile of sympathetic understanding: Geekie was not like himself, an Ishmael, but he was the athletic butt of Tads', an Ishmael and a mock: they ought to get on well together!

'If you chaps are willing, we will put in as much private practice as possible,' went on McPhail; 'this field is two miles away from the shop, and no one is likely to come this way. When you are proficient I will make it my business to acquaint Stanhope with the fact. I will guarantee that then you will both be tried again in the house team.'

'Private training?' gasped Geekie, but Vassall already had a glimmering of the idea which was at the back of Peter McPhail's prolific mind.

'You have both weaknesses,' explained McPhail ruthlessly; 'you, Geek, old horse, leave the behind you when you run—in fact, you have practically no ball-control whatever; and Vassall— well, Vassall will agree that he also has something to learn, I think?'

'I agree,' replied Vassall. In such a company he was willing to confess his outstanding fault, shameful as it was.

'All right! We're all agreed. Now we'll start with you first, Geekie— ever heard of a winger called William Meredith?'

Geekie's face glowed at the mention of his hero.

'Of course! I've got his life—with diagrams and photographs and things—back at the shop! Do you know how he learnt ball-control, Mac? He dribbled round sticks placed in the ground!'

34

'We haven't got sticks to-day, but we can collect stones; off with you!' ordered McPhail peremptorily.

The self-appointed trainer had his schedule already planned. He made Geekie indulge in dribbling practice for fifteen minutes by the watch. Then he walked across to Vassall.

'Geekie and I are both going to tackle you—we are backs, you understand, and you are a centre-forward. There is the goal,' he pointed to a space marked by two large stones. 'We shan't be gentle,' he added; 'at least, I shan't.'

Vassall nodded.

'Now, Geekie, you have changed yourself through force of circumstances from an outside-right into a left-back,' said McPhail. 'Vassall here is a centre-forward—a dangerous man who must be stopped at all costs. Go back six paces, Vassall, and then try to dribble your way through us.'

A quarter of an hour of this mimic football strife, and then McPhail took up a position between the two large stones which he had said represented goal-posts.

'Practise shooting!' he ordered; 'get out on right there, Geekie, and send over the very best centre you can.'

It was hard work, for Geekie's centring left much to be desired, and there was no one behind "goal" to fag the ball.

But McPhail felt himself well repaid. Vassall might never be able to cure himself of that amazing funking—he had shirked being charged by Geekie even! —but he was a masterpiece when it came to trapping ball and shooting. Once Geekie had contrived to lob over a dropping centre. Moving leisurely, Vassall had got his instep to the ball and it whizzed past McPhail at an incredible speed.

'Practise! Practise! Practise!' as the great Bill says,' commented McPhail, looking at his watch; on the whole, I am not entirely dissatisfied with this afternoon's work.' And, unlacing the ball, he deflated it and restored the remains to his overcoat pocket.

'*Allons!*' he cried, and the strangely-assorted trio walked back to Repington.

CHAPTER VIII

Tads Feels Justified

David Vassall was the busiest fellow at Repington. What with practising boxing with Benny Bennison, practising football arts and crafts under the tutelage of Peter McPhail, he had little time to worry about the stigma attached to him. But the shame was still corroding his soul.

One afternoon he arrived at the boxing gymnasium to find Bennison boxing with a sturdily-built youngster, who possessed a decidedly snub nose and a very pugnacious assortment of other features.

'Kid Kerry,' announced the ex-champion with a wave of the hand, 'a likely lad. He's come along to have a spar with you this afternoon, Mr. Vassall.'

'Chawmed, ah'm sure!' grinned Kerry, the Kid, holding out a knobbly fist. 'Nobby Durrance is a pal o' mine,' he announced with another grin.

This might have been bad news to David Vassall. Nobby Durrance was the bellicose butcher's boy who had precipitated the spirited passage-at-arms that had led to the Head of Repington placing the town out of bounds recently. But, instead of feeling depressed, Vassall experienced a strange exhilaration run through him at the words. He could scarcely understand it, but only knew it was so.

'Yes,' said Kid Kerry (Joe Smith when at home!) 'I happened to meet Nobby on the way 'ere this afternoon, and 'e sent 'is very kind regards.'

'Not so much talk there, Kid,' admonished Bennison, 'here are the gloves, Mr. Vassall.'

Whilst Vassall was preparing for the fray, Bennison gave him some interesting information. This, summarized, was to the effect that the time had come, in the opinion of the instructor, when Vassall should get some sparring practice with a boy of about his own weight. That was why he had kept Kid Kerry on the premises that afternoon.

'Goin' in for the game as a pro, the Kid is,' whispered Bennison, his voice hoarse with excitement. 'He's very fast and tricky—watch him closely, Mr. Vassall, and he'll learn you a lot.'

Vassall had already absorbed a good deal of knowledge from the hands of the illustrious Bennison. He had mastered the first elements of boxing—he could now defend himself with a fair measure of success, and was able to take advantage of any opening which simply yawned before him. Beyond that, however, he had not progressed.

How sadly deficient his education was still, he realized early in the first of the three rounds he had with the obliging Kid Kerry that afternoon. Kerry was a mocking shadow—but a shadow that had two very painful fists which rattled home on all parts of his face, shoulders, and chest. It was disheartening trying to check or avoid that stream of blows, but there were two factors which forced Vassall to keep his ground as well as was possible. The first was the consciousness that he simply dared not give in or show that he was afraid, and the second was that he was encouraged all the time by Benny Bennison.

'You're doin' fine, sir,' Bennison said, when he rallied after an especially furious assault by the budding professional; 'mind that right! Now, sir—shoot in your left!'

Panting, with blood streaming from a cut on the mouth, and with his left eye showing distinct signs of mourning, Vassall staggered to a seat at the end of the second round. He was thankful of the one minute break. But at the same time he was aware that both Bennison and Kid Kerry were watching him closely. Kerry had played with him. He knew that—played with him as a cat plays with a mouse. The other had not been unnecessarily brutal—no doubt Bennison would have stopped him from being that—but he had been slyly malicious; he had promised his pal Nobby, obviously, that he would take it out of this school kid, he was to avenge the damage done to Nobby's some-what prominent nose on the last occasion that town and school had come into conflict.

'Time!' called Bennison.

Kerry commenced to circle round Vassall with a cat-like glide. His eyes were shining, and there was still that mocking smile on his coarse but good-natured face

Smack!

That evil right of his crept up under the school-boy's guard, drawing more blood. Vassall staggered, and then an inward force, which he could not understand, drove him back to the attack. There was a sneer on Kid Kerry's face as he waited. "Come and be slaughtered!" it said plainly.

But, subtle as Kerry was, he made a miscalculation now. He ignored the possibilities in his opponent's left hand and paid the penalty, for, amid the jubilant exclamations of Bennison, Vassall managed to land a very workmanlike left jab—and not only to land it, but to plant it where it would do the most good—flush upon the square jaw.

'Bravo, sir!' called Bennison, dancing with glee, and then the next minute, and in a different tone: 'Mind your guard now—ah! I told you to be careful, sir!'

Something had hit him with the seeming force of a sledge-hammer, and Vassall fell backwards. Kid Kerry had resented the liberty taken with his chin, and had rushed in hot-headed to the attack, both arms swinging sledge-hammer fashion. One of these blows had "connected".

Bennison rushed to the schoolboy's assistance.

'You're not badly hurt, I hope, Mr. Vassall?'

Vassall swallowed something, and then managed to reply: 'No—and I want to stick it out.'

He stuck it out. What is more, from now until the end of the round Kid Kerry was not able to land another blow. The reason was a surprising one—Vassall took up the offensive, and Kerry's attention was fully occupied in protecting himself.

Vassall seemed possessed of a demon. He wanted to hit the other—hit, and hurt him. He wanted to knock the mocking smile off the face of Nobby's pal; he wanted—*how* he wanted!—to justify himself in the eyes of his tutor.

He had his reward for hard striving. When Benny Bennison rubbed him down, Kid Kerry having gone to the shower, the ex-pugilist said: 'You've got guts, Mr. Vassall—guts, and a nice straight left. Never mind the rest; that'll come. And now I've got some-thing to ask you.'

'Geek, old horse,' said Peter McPhail, 'is it true that you have a trusty relative in the town?'

'An uncle—an absolute worm!' vouchsafed the youth who could mop up maths to the bewilderment of all the masters at Repington. 'Why?'

'Worm he may be, worm let him be but you've got to wangle a written invitation out of him for next Tuesday evening! "Dine and spend the evening" sort of thing. And not only for yourself, but for friend Vassall and little me. See to it, Tig!'

'But I hate the perisher!' protested Geekie; 'he's the biggest bore in the world. Talks about nothing but political economy and all that rot! I loathe going to see him; he can't talk decently about any one sport! That's why he never writes to me.'

McPhail drew his arm through the taller boy's.

'Listen, child!' he said, in the manner of a fond but indulgent father advising a wayward son; 'let not the sun go down upon your wrath this night. Speed thee to the perisher, and say unto him: Uncle, I have come of my own free will and accord to make what amends may be possible for my neglect. I have misunderstood your nature; I have under-estimated your sterling qualities. Behold, then, I have returned, your prodigal nephew—and now get on with the fatted calf business! I'm bringing two pals to grub next Tuesday evening!'

"Is it really important, Mac?' inquired Geekie, who would have led the way through devouring flames for the junior's sake.

'Urgently, vitally important. Bend down, you ungainly giraffe, and I will impart news of great import.'

A few moments later Geekie was hurtling his Ion: legs in the direction of the town.

'Oh, Watney,' called Tads.

I limped up to the house-master.

Tads smiled. 'There's a bit of a boxing show of to-night down in the town; I think, if no word of it gets about, that I might relax the bonds of discipline sufficiently to ask if you would care to come with me. I tell you what: you come to dinner, and it doesn't matter to anyone else how we spend the rest of the evening, does it?'

'I should think not, sir.' I smiled too. Tads was the finest sportsman I had ever met. When he found that a fellow was worthy of being taken into his confidence, he treated him as a friend. The highest honour that any of us in the house knew was to be invited to dine with Tads: going to the Head's place was nothing to it, although Mildmay wasn't a bad chap off duty.

I dined with Tads that night without saying a word to anyone, and then we slipped off down town. Of course there was nothing wrong in it, but Tads was laughing and joking like a schoolboy himself.

'That fellow Bennison, ex-champion Middle weight of England he used to be, you know, has sent me word that he is giving a semi-private show of some of his pupils at the Exeter Hall to-night,' he said, as we turned into the High Street.

I had always been keen on boxing and I was looking forward to the show, but my keenness was nothing, compared to Tads'. Boxing and football: these were his twin passions.

Having gained two seats near the ringside, Tad changed the conversation.

'We don't seem to be in for much of a football season, Watney—pity about that fellow Vassall. Have you any ideas on the subject?'

'Yes, sir—but I may be wrong. Do you mind if I keep them to myself a little longer?'

Curious how one hugs a mystery, however small, to oneself! I had heard of the mysterious afternoon disappearances of Vassall in company with McPhail and Geekie, and had speculated what could be in the wind. I didn't want to be premature, especially with a man like Tads. Much better to let any development occur quite unexpectedly.

'Certainly!' replied Tads, answering me; 'as a matter of fact, I have a theory about Vassall myself. Pity he funks, though.'

Then a man, who looked something like a battered bulldog (that was how his appearance struck me), climbed into the ring. He nodded affably to Tads and smiled as he did so.

'That's Bennison—a thoroughly good sort,' re-marked the housemaster: 'I've had many a good spar with him.'

'Gen'l'men,' said the man in the ring, 'it is very kind of you, I'm sure, to be here this evening in answer to my invitation. I think I can promise you some fair sport. There are one or two very likely lads training with me at the present time.

'The first bout,' turning in our direction, 'is one of three two-minute rounds between Kid Kerry and,' looking it seemed to me very hard at Tads, 'a boy of the name of young Vassall.'

Tads straightened himself up in his chair. 'Vassall, did he say, Watney?' he inquired, and then, before I could reply, we both saw something which paralysed us with astonishment.

Leading a small procession of three boys came McPhail. The figure was unmistakably McPhail, even though he moved in such strange and unexpected surroundings. He was clad in white flannel trousers and wore a cricket sweater. He carried a large sponge one hand, whilst a heavy towel hung over his left arm.

Behind McPhail stalked a yet more remarks figure.

'Surely—surely that's Geekie?' exclaimed Tads. He rubbed his eyes as though he could scarcely credit own vision.

'It appears to me, sir, to be Geekie—undoubtedly,' I replied.

Just then Geekie, dressed like McPhail in cricket flannels and sweater, caught sight of us. He communicated his alarm to McPhail by first catching hold of his arm, and then whispering feverishly into other's ear.

The astonishing McPhail behaved as anyone who knew him would naturally have expected him to behave. He turned to the last boy in the procession—it was Vassall, as both Tads and I had expected by this time, of course—and held a quick and animated conversation with him. The end of this talk saw McPhail and Vassall coming towards us.

'Good evening, sir,' said McPhail, addressing Tads.

'Vassall and I are surprised to see you—but very glad all the same. Vassall, acting on my advice, has taken up boxing under a thoroughly

40

good man—you will be bound to remember the name, sir—Bennison: he was Middle-weight Champion of Great Britain, 1920-1914—even if you do not know the man himself. He had the chance to make his first public —or semi-public—appearance to-night against a good performer, and I strongly advised him to accept it. The responsibility is all mine, sir, and I am perfectly willing to take it—but you will let him box, sir?'

Tads—what a sportsman!—turned to Vassall.

'Your opponent is already in the ring, Vassall,' he said; 'I wish you luck.'

Vassall's handsome face flushed as he turned away.

'You don't know anything about this, I suppose, Watney?' demanded Tads.

'Not a thing, sir. All I know is that McPhail has constituted himself a sort of guide, philosopher, and friend to Vassall, a fellow who is two years older than himself at least, and that he has developed some scheme in regard to Vassall.'

'Entirely characteristic of McPhail as I know him,' commented Tads, 'but Geekie? What is George Gregory Geekie doing in that galley, Watney?'

'I don't understand Geekie's position myself, sir, but the three are always about together now. No doubt McPhail has an idea about Geekie, also.'

'H'm! They're going to box.'

I knew then that it was required of me to keep silent—until the end of the first round, at least.

To say that I was astonished at the show which Vassall put up is to express myself mildly. His opponent, although quite young, was a hard-bitten looking customer, a professional fighter in the making I judged him to be, and he was obviously out to floor Vassall at the first opportunity. But Vassall had boxing defence which must have been built up for him by sound tuition, and although he got considerably the worst of each round, and lost rather heavily on points in the end, his display was distinctly creditable.

Sensing something of the drama which I knew must be hidden behind Vassall's strange appearance that evening, I watched the proceedings seriously. Had I not been serious I must have laughed at the demeanour of McPhail. The latter acted as Vassall's chief second (Geekie was his assistant—hence the white flannels and sweaters, of course) and he performed his duties with tremendous gravity. He fanned, sponged, and advised with as much earnestness as though his charge was boxing for the championship of the world.

When Bennison, acting as referee, signalled the end of the last round, McPhail, piloting Vassall, came to speak to Tads again.

'Vassall will do better than this, sir,' he remarked 'Of course, this is his first try-out before spectators. Benny Bennison thought it would give him experience to box before a crowd—even if it were only a small one. That is why we came here to-night. He wants experience badly.'

'The invitation from Geekie's uncle, Professor Annan?' asked Tads.

'Oh, that was genuine enough, sir! We did dine at the professor's, but came on here afterwards. As I said just now, I accept the full responsibility.'

'I possibly will remember that, McPhail. In the meantime, you may reflect upon the wisdom contained in the adage about a still tongue making wise head.'

'Oh, thanks *awfully*, sir!' cried McPhail, and led his two companions away.

'Watney,' said Tads, as he left the hall, 'I think I shall feel justified in not making any further reference to this matter. After all, it was a very pleasant evening. But what do you imagine that youngster McPhail meant when he said Vassall wanted boxing experience badly?'

'He probably intends Vassall to enter for the house boxing competition, sir,' I suggested.

'Ah! Then that would mean he would come up against Birtles.'

'No doubt McPhail had that in mind, sir.'

'Watney,' concluded Tads, moderating his fine stride to my lamentable hobble, 'if nothing occurs to stop his intellectual growth, McPhail will be a great man one day.'

CHAPTER IX

The Unseen Watcher

Stanhope, Footer Captain of Tads, was not himself. He was worried, and worry can play the dickens with the most equable of temperaments. Not that Stanhope, a most energetic individual, a fellow who took his onerous office very seriously, could be said to be the possessor of an equable temperament at any time—but now he was even more on edge than usual. As the advertisements say, there was a reason.

Being the skipper of a footer team is a delightful occupation in theory. In practice the thing never works out quite so well. The glad hurrahs are too often drowned by the groans of criticism. Stanhope had had plenty of chance, although the term was only a few weeks old, of discovering this immortal truth for himself.

Frankly, the team had been most disappointing. Up to a point it had promised fairly well, although in order to be on the safe side he had been gloomy-minded at the opening meeting of the committee. It was true that Morris, Winter, and Stephenson had gone from the previous season's team and that Huish was away ill with appendicitis, but still there were Jenkins, Bridges, Birtles, and himself left. The trouble was that none of the new material had turned out much use.

The defence wasn't so bad—in fact Jenkins and Birtles were almost certain to be considered by Manners, the School Skipper, when he came to pick his team, but the forward line was—punk. Bridges had a hopeless task: he had little or no support, and he couldn't expect to go through a side on his own.

Centre-forward and outside-right were the two positions that had to be filled—or rather re-filled. Both fellows tried had proved hopeless.

It was mainly due to the deplorable weakness forward that Tads' was still without a victory. It had played two house matches to date, losing to Dormer's 2-1 (the memory of this still made Stanhope writhe), and drawing with Hopwood's 0–0. It should have won the latter game easily, for it pressed almost continuously in the second half, whilst Hopwood's never once looked like getting past Merrick, Jenkins, and Birtles; but even Bridges got affected by the general rot, actually missing a penalty! It was true that the offence for which the spot-kick had been awarded was a mild affair—a very doubtful case of "hands" on the part of Ottaway, the left-back, but the fact remained that Tads' had been awarded a penalty—and had failed to score even from that. Bridges had not been able to give any coherent excuse why he missed, sending the ball high over the bar, but that scarcely helped matters.

Stanhope had not had sufficient experience of life to know that many earthly ambitions have a habit of becoming illusive. Even if such knowledge had been his, he would have declared it poor consolation. He had counted so much upon getting his house in the van; it was agonizing to find the once proud cock house now occupying the humiliating position of an "also-ran."

This particular afternoon he was so fed up with the general outlook that he declined joining Bridges Jenkins on the touch-line to watch the Canaver's-Moody's house match, and strolled off by himself.

A centre-forward and an outside-right! As other men have longed for the mythical Elixir of Life, the Magic Philosopher's Stone, or the fabled wealth of the Incas, so did Stanhope now long to set eyes upon two fellows wearing Tads' House caps who might ever approximate to being a centre-forward and an outside-right.

He walked on and on; came to a network of cross-roads; saw a stile; climbed it, and then heard unmistakable bouncing of a football.

At the precise moment that he heard the food bouncing, Stanhope was standing in a small clearing. When he saw what was happening, he secluded him: behind a hedge.

His astonishment was so profound that he could only stare in uncomprehending amazement for some time. There were three fellows in the smallish field before him—and they all belonged to Tads'.

This fact was extraordinary enough in itself, but Stanhope had fresh wonders over which to ponder. The three boys were McPhail, his fag, Geekie—jumping snakes, Geekie!—and Vassall. Vassall, the football funk-shy!

What on earth were they doing? McPhail stood between a couple of huge stones, and, as the unseen watcher gasped, his fag kicked the football, which a moment before he had been holding in his hands, out to Geekie. The latter was standing wide to the right of McPhail, and not far from Stanhope himself.

'Trap it first time, Geek!' came the command in McPhail's unmistakable voice—and while Stanhope's eyes nearly left his head with a sort of strangling surprise, Geekie *did* trap it first time. Moreover, in what seemed almost the same action, he swept the ball forward, motioned with his left hand—and sent over a really magnificent centre. This was met by Vassall, who came running up, and nodded neatly past McPhail's outstretched hands.

'They're practising!' Stanhope told his immortal soul. 'What !'

But he had no time to finish the sentence. 'Once more, Geek!' called McPhail, and again the same manoeuvre was gone through. Geekie might have known that he was being watched by critical eyes, for again he trapped the ball with scrupulous care and wielded his long right leg with artistic effect. This time his centre came ankle-high to Vassall standing in the "goal mouth," but, getting his foot to the ball, Vassall banged it past McPhail without any apparent effort.

'This must be a dream!' whispered Stanhope to himself; 'I've been thinking about the team so much that I'm seeing things.' But, pinching himself to be on the safe side, and to make sure, he finally came to the conclusion that the scene in front of him was not a delusion but an actual fact. Bewildering!

He was bound to wait. He saw Vassall practise shooting, sending in long low powerful shots that came off his boot like a bullet from a gun; he watched Vassall attempt to dribble past both Geekie and McPhail (who had changed apparently from a goalkeeper into a back for this special stunt); he saw Geekie's long, awkward body hurl itself at Vassall in a good old-fashioned, robust charge, and just miss its object because Vassall had swerved away; finally he watched McPhail and the others take off their footer boots, wrap them into a parcel, and then deflate the ball. To conclude his afternoon's entertainment, Stanhope heard his fag say with obvious glee: 'Methinks, Messieurs, we shall have a little surprise waiting for someone one of these days. The hour is drawing nigh!'

Stanhope crouched low to avoid being seen, watched the three conspirators fade away in the distance—and then heaved an enormous sigh. 'Well, I'll be jiggered!' he exclaimed.

Vassall fumbled with the handle of the door before he entered. He was extremely nervous, and his hand shook. The stentorian "Come!" which had greeted his first hesitant knock had unnerved him. Now he was sorely tempted to turn tail and run. Only the fact that he knew McPhail would be in the room beyond kept him true to his resolve. That and the fact that he had promised.

The footer captain of Tads' looked up in surprise at his visitor.

'You want to see me?' he asked. His tone was coldly impersonal.

'Yes, Stanhope—if you don't mind.'

'Mind! Well, you're here now, so that doesn't matter, in any case. What do you want?'

It was not very encouraging, and Vassall wished that the floor might open and swallow him. But he had to go through with it; after all the fellow could only refuse him.

'I want to ask you a favour, Stanhope,' he said, nervously; 'I want you to give me another trial at footer.'

'Rather a dangerous experiment for me to make —don't you agree?'

'I do!' The tone was wholly sincere. 'I know I was a rotten failure, Stanhope, I know that I let the whole house down. I'm sorry.'

'We were all sorry, Vassall—sorry that a chap belonging to Tads' should have been known as a funk throughout the shop! It was—horrible! And now you want me to run the risk again!—you must see for yourself that it would be a risk?'

'Yes—it would be a risk,' agreed the supplicant frankly.

'Then ?'

'Because I want to have another chance to get hold of myself, Stanhope. I swear to you I'll do everything I possibly can not to funk,' replied Vassall, answering the question before it was spoken.

'He's really good at shooting,' put in McPhail, appearing from behind a screen.

Stanhope wheeled.

'How do *you* know?' he demanded. 'Vassall hasn't played footer since —since that day—'

'No, I'd forgotten that,' replied McPhail, slowly winking at Vassall, who wasn't in the mood just then to appreciate such a pleasantry.

Silence fell. McPhail knew when to talk and when to keep quiet. This was essentially a period to be set apart for private meditation, he decided. Besides, his real chance would come later. Stanhope did not speak because he was thinking hard, and Vassall was too nervous to press his case any more.

In the end:

'Well, Vassall, the most I can do is to say that I will consider what you have told me,' Stanhope said; 'mind, I'm not promising anything!'

'Thanks very much,' stammered the applicant, and nervously vanished.

'How do you know that Vassall, although a funk, is a good shot?' demanded the Footer Captain of his fag.

McPhail became one of those "who only stand and wait." He was bursting with the thoroughly understandable desire to tell the whole thrilling story. But for the solemn promise he had made Vassall to say nothing to anyone, he would have made his dramatic disclosure. As it was—

'Well, he looks as though he can, anyway!' he declared with a show of defiance.

Stanhope turned away to hide a smile. If McPhail was not prepared to give him his confidence, he would not drag it from him. He could guess that his fag was playing a joke off on him, but as this was for the benefit of the house team he was quite prepared forgive it.

McPhail fidgeted. While he had conquered the desire to tell his secret, yet his curiosity as to the skipper's intentions was uncontrollable.

'What are you going to do?' he asked.

Stanhope's reply was brief and decisive.

'I'm going to wait until Jenkins and Bridges roll up,' he said. 'Whether your pal, Vassall, gets another chance will be settled by voting.'

Someone said that the list for the house team again Lorimer's was up, and there was a frantic rush made.

The crush was terrific, and this became more pronounced when a junior near the board shouted in high, hysterical voice: 'I say, they're playing the funk-shy!'

'Vassall?' screamed a dozen voices; 'oh, my eye!'

'You can't see straight, Timmins!' scoffed Tidmarsh.

The boy with the maligned optic vision pointed with a trembling finger.

'It's on the board, you ass!—look for yourself, then!'

'Vassall's in!'

There was surprise, incredulity almost, certainly disgust, and a splash of indignation in the comments. The inconceivable had happened. What could Stanhope be thinking about? To play a fellow who had obviously funked!—who had made the name of the best house in the shop smell to high Heaven——! Forthwith an emergency meeting of indignant protestors was held.

Into this hurly-burly Stanhope came striding.

'Out of the way, you kids!' he called good-humouredly.

'I say, Stanhope, you're playing *Vassall!*' cried Tidmarsh, all other considerations ignored and forgotten in the overwhelming dismay of the moment.

The skipper's face clouded.

'The chap had to have a second chance,' he said, as though speaking to himself.

That appealed to the sporting instincts of the critics, and Stanhope walked away in silence.

Then another honoured member of the house team came along.

'I say, Birtles, they're playing Vassall!' piped Tidmarsh again; 'we've just been speaking to Stanhope about it, and he says he had to give the chap a second chance!'

'What for?—to make the house a general laughing-stock again, I suppose?'

Although he was respected for his football, Birtles was not otherwise popular. He sneered, and had an unpleasant practice of bullying in subtle, but cruel, ways. But Tidmarsh, encouraged by the success of his first remark, went on:

'Don't you think it's rotten, Birtles, to play a funk-like Vassall again?'

'Decidedly rotten!' answered Birtles. 'A funk can ruin the play of a whole team!' He had raised his voice—purposely, it would seem.

The next moment a gasp rose from the juniors' ranks. Round the corner came the very man they had been criticizing. By Vassall's side was McPhail.

Silence fell like a blanket. It was a moment of tense emotion, of strained attention and expectant drama. Vassall's face was white, but he bore himself well. Quite obviously he knew that he was under discussion. Quite obviously he had heard the last remark made by Birtles.

Neither he nor McPhail gave any sign. They attempted to walk through the crowd as though the latter did not exist. Only when he reached the side of Tidmarsh, the talkative junior, did McPhail make a start.

'Why, that must be the team!' he said, as though the idea had just occurred to him; 'I'll catch you up, Vassall.'

There was not a break in McPhail's voice and scarcely a hint of excitement. He was just mildly curious, that was all.

Vassall was not such a good actor. Stanhope had not spoken to him since he had made his appeal to the Footer Captain. He really did not know whether he had been picked to play or not. The fact that he believed he had been picked sent him into a state of the wildest excitement. But he had walked away from the notice-board because he knew it would be the rankest bad form for him to evidence the slightest curiosity.

'You're playing, Vassall!'

McPhail made the statement nonchalantly.

'What! You don't mean to say that you're a footballer, Vassall?'

Birtles' words were heavy with malice. Someone among the juniors sniggered shrilly.

'Birtles' Beers for Bloated Blighters!' chanted a voice, blithe and gay, 'my word, Birtles, you're getting to look more like a bottle of stout than ever! Heavy and heady, you know!'

Like a great many people who never scrupled to study other persons' feelings, Birtles was abnormally sensitive himself. He hated to lose any of his (believed) impressive dignity. In his early days at Repington the fact that his father was a well-known brewer had caused him to be greeted with the cry of "Birtles' bottled beers!" It had taken him some time to live the horror down. But he believed he had done it: this term not once so far had the words seared his sensitive soul.

Bellowing like a bull, he made a frantic rush at McPhail. The latter ducked, and someone stood in front to guard him. The blow which had been aimed at McPhail would have struck Vassall if the latter had not guarded himself.

'Out of the way—you!' roared Birtles.

Vassall remained perfectly still—very pale, but also very determined.

'Take it yourself, then!' cried Birtles, launching another blow.

This, like the first, was guarded, and then Birtles, completely overcome by rage, rushed forward, his hands groping for the other's neck. The next moment two desperately struggling figures were swaying this way and that, while the startled juniors looked fascinatedly on.

'Stop that!

Tads, authoritative, commanding, had come upon the scene without being noticed. He caught the shoulders of the contestants and prised them apart.

'Birtles!—Vassall!' he said.

Nothing more was required. That was why Tads did not ask any questions.

The juniors drifted away: Birtles slouched off by himself. Vassall remained near McPhail.

'I see you're playing against Lorimer's, Vassall,' commented Tads.

'Yes, sir,' replied the football funk-shy, flushing.

CHAPTER X

The Game with Lorimer's

The whole school turned out to watch Tads' play Lorimer's. It happened that there was no other match of any importance on that day. That was one factor, of course, but an even more important one was that every house in the shop was intrigued by the news that Stanhope had decided to play the funk-shy, who had become the Ishmael of his house, at centre-forward, in the desperate endeavour to improve his team.

'I shall see you this afternoon, Watney—of course,' Tads had remarked after morning school, and I had hobbled out with him. We found the touch-lines and the backs of the goals crowded; fellows were standing three and four deep. For the interest which was being shown it might have been a school match.

'I hope Vassall will stand the ordeal,' Tads said quietly, and I guessed that his feelings were something akin to my own. We both wished the centre-forward to come through with credit, but we were afraid—for myself, I scarcely knew of what. It seemed ridiculous to have any doubts about a boy whom we had seen stand up in a boxing ring and take heavy punishment, but there it was. You see, neither of us had been able to solve the Vassall enigma as yet.

When Vassall turned out with the rest of Tads' team, walking by himself, a perceptible wave of excitement could be seen passing through the crowd. Within my recollection of Repington no new boy had created so much interest in himself as had Vassall—unless I cite McPhail—and, of course, McPhail was an oddity, a phenomenon. The fact that the interest in Vassall was of the morbid rather than the healthy character accentuated rather than otherwise the attention of the school.

Vassall was the man then on whom all eyes were turned. That he was the son of one who had cause glorious chapters to be written in Repington football history was known by this time throughout the shop. The fellow looked white and strained.

Stanhope lost the toss, and had to kick against the wind. Vassall tapped to Bridges, the latter back-heeled to Stanhope, the skipper swung out to his right wing—and the game was on.

A tall, ungainly form swept the ball before him, and was off down the touch-line like a greyhound. At least, the simile might have been permitted if the winger had run with more grace.

'This Geekie business is almost as astounding Vassall's,' Tads said.

I looked again. The outside-right was Geekie! My attention had been so concentrated on Vassall up till now that I had scarcely given a thought to the rest of the team. I had even forgotten the seething excitement, not unmixed with derision—with which the selection of Geekie had been greeted by the house.

'He couldn't be much worse than Thompson anyway,' was the crisp comment of one critic—Garraway, I think it was—and after that there seemed nothing more to be said.

'Why—he's *good!*' cried someone near us incredulously.

Marvel of marvels, Geekie was good! He had swept past the left-half like a runaway train, had resisted the challenge of Bevin, Lorimer's left-back, and had still retained the ball. (The old Geekie would have lost it long before!)

'Oh, well centred, sir!'

Geekie might still be a butt, but the tribute came spontaneously from all parts of the ground. On the very bye-line the new outside right had steadied himself and had planted the ball with splendid accuracy right into the goal mouth.

What followed was watched with eager eyes. I felt myself thrilling with excitement. A boy with smooth dark hair came rushing up. Judging the dropping centre well, he got his head to the ball and nodded it deftly sideways.

'Goal!' cried many.

But Lorimer's goalkeeper, leaping high, just managed to get his right hand to the ball. With as much craftsmanship as luck—or so it seemed to me—he tipped that danger-laden ball over the bar. It had been a magnificent piece of work by all concerned.

'That was Vassall,' said Tads, while rapturous cheering smote the throbbing air, and his voice was glad. 'I think he must be a footballer in spite of everything.'

Layton, the outside-left, placed the corner well, but it was cleared. Still, we of Tads' were well content. If that early burst was to be relied upon, it meant that we had discovered a right-winger and a centre-forward. And the outside-right was Geekie, the former butt of the house, and the centre-forward was the Ishmael!

'Come along, Lorimer's!'

The eager shouts of their supporters seemed to bring home to our opponents how near they had been to disaster. Campion, the inside-right, and the captain of the side, took advantage of the ball going into touch to speak animatedly to Padmore, his centre-half, and Bartlett the left-half. The latter moved to Geekie's side—and stayed there. No more touch-line flashes on the part of this astonishing, be-spectacled outside-right if he could help it.

As for Padmore, Lorimer's centre-half, he rolled up his sleeves afresh.

It did not require much intelligence to sense what that action meant; the hint it intended to convey. Padmore was going to act on the instructions he had received from his skipper—he was going to do his best to squash the opposing centre-forward into complete ineffectiveness. He had been caught napping once, but he would see that it didn't occur again. If Vassal had scored through that header—

Padmore was possibly the heaviest fellow at Repington; he must have weighed every ounce of twelve stone. The astonishing thing was that, carrying so much weight, he could cover the ground so well. He had an extremely awkward style, but he was a good centre-half; in fact, there were even divided opinions about him and Stanhope, who was the school's pivot. Some went so far as to say that—and they weren't all Lorimer's fellows—he was a better man than the Tads' skipper. Personally, I did not agree to this view, all sentiment apart, for, if Padmore was more robust and possibly a shade more difficult to get past, Stanhope was an incomparably better purveyor for his forwards.

Still, the malicious fates must have grinned, for there was one fellow playing football at Repington who could be safely depended upon to test a centre-forward's nerve that chap was Padmore of Lorimer's!

In the early excitement caused by Geekie's startling run down the wing, and Vassall's spectacular attempt to score by means of that brilliant header, the centre-forward's besetting weakness had no doubt been temporarily forgotten by the crowd.

But when a minute after Padmore had been seen to roll up his sleeves, Stanhope, dribbling through a ruck of players, sped a beautiful ball forward with the sharp cry—'*Vassall!*' the horror that I had hoped never to see again reared its poisonous head once more.

Vassall took the pass splendidly, but out of the corner of his eye he must have seen Padmore tearing down on him.

I could see him waver. He tried to control himself, but in that instant when he should either have endeavoured to swerve past the centre-half, or meet his charge shoulder to shoulder, he—sheered away!

'No question about that, unfortunately,' said Tads, 'really, Watney, it's too bad—but I don't think the chap can help it.'

'I'm fairly certain he can't, sir; if it were purely a question of plain funk—cowardice—he wouldn't have taken up boxing.'

'No—I agree there. The nuisance is that, as I said before, he's a natural footballer. Oh, I wish those fellows wouldn't shout!'

But, of course, the crowd *did* shout—

'Don't let him frighten you, Vassall! Play up!— don't funk, Vassall!'

There was not so much bitterness as might have been expected. The crowd still remembered the opening bit of play, I supposed. But still the cries hurt.

'They'll only make him worse!' said Tads.

That was obvious. Vassall was fidgeting frightfully. When the ball came to him he flicked it away at once.

Now about that same flick: the fellow who has football in him shows it by the merest touch; he has only to let his boot slide over a football to demonstrate his innate skill. Although Vassall had been painfully anxious to get rid of the ball on account of his nervousness, it travelled fast and true to Bridges. The ball might have been carried to the inside-left.

'Yes, the fellow's a footballer!' said Tads again. 'Oh, well played, Bridges!'

"Bumper" Bridges, who played inside left for the school as well as for Tads', had concluded a magnificent dribble with a shot that grazed the crossbar. Six inches lower, and we should inevitably have scored.

"Bumper"—hence his nickname—was no light-weight, and just before he had shot he had "bumped" into Padmore with a force that staggered both of them.

While the cheers broke out again, a voice called: 'See how Bridges does it, Vassall! Don't be frightened!'

It was pitiable. If the crowd wished the funk-shy to forget himself they were adopting the worst possible methods. One could almost see Vassall's nerves vibrating. It reminded me all over again of that wretched afternoon when he first played.

From the goal-kick, Campion started a hot raid. Dribbling cleverly, he drew our left-half, and then sent out to his wing. The outside-right held the ball long enough to get Birtles in two minds, and then suddenly raced towards the corner-flag.

Birtles, his annoyance clearly imprinted on his face, pelted after him and made a desperate lunge. So desperate was his tackle that he slipped before he reached his opponent, and the Lorimer's winger had a clear course.

'Lorimer's! Lorimer's! Well played, Thompson! Centre, man!'

Thompson might have been excused if he had lost his head. He showed his playing worth by coaxing Jenkins, our right-back into tackling him, and then slipped the ball to the waiting Campion. Merrick rushed out —but the ball sped past him to the net at the back of the goal.

Lorimer's were one up!

This was a bitter disappointment to our contingent. The goal had been cleverly obtained and well deserved, but Tads' had done the bulk of the pressing up till now. The knowledge rankled.

'Oh, come along, Tads'!'

There was almost a despairing wail in the exhortations. Cock house at footer the year before and now everybody seemed able to beat us! The battle waged more or less evenly after this until half-time, and then Stanhope, seeing us, walked across. Tads drew the skipper away from the crowd.

'It's no use putting Bridges into the centre, I suppose?' asked Tads.

'It will weaken the left wing,' replied Stanhope gravely; 'of course, if you think it would be best, sir—Bridges *might* be able to get through.' Stanhope looked at me, and then went on: 'I am afraid I did wrong in playing Vassall again, sir.'

'He's a player, Stanhope.'

'Oh, he's jolly good at trapping the ball when there's no one on him!' replied the captain bitterly, 'but you saw him funk Padmore, sir?'

'Yes. It's a pity. I don't think he can help it. I was saying so to Watney just now. Watney agrees with me.'

Stanhope threw away the piece of lemon he had been sucking.

'Can't help funking, sir?' he said incredulously, and then, the whistle going, he did not finish, but walked back to the field, shaking his head, plainly puzzled and highly indignant.

'Stanhope doesn't understand, Watney,' said Tads, and I nodded. I didn't understand myself very clearly, and I sympathized with Stanhope. If it had not been for the fellow's boxing, the thing would have been simple enough; as it was, it was jolly difficult. The man was plucky in one sport, and funked in another. What could anyone have made of it?

Vassall behaved in the same fashion in the second half as he had in the first. So long as he had plenty of room in which to move he was clever, almost superlatively clever, with the ball. But, to put it mildly, he still shirked physical contact with Padmore, or, indeed, with any of his opponents.

Fortunately, ten minutes after the re-start, Bridges attracted all the attention to himself by ramming home a good centre of Geekie's— Geekie was the surprise of the match, let me tell you: fast, fairly plucky and a sender-over of capital centres—and, the score level, the crowd got into a better temper.

Having equalized, it was only natural that Tads' should wish to win. Human nature that, of course.

'One more, Tads'!' shouted our supporters in frantic excitement.

The play after this became desperately ding-dong. First Lorimer's pressed, and were beaten off by a determined defence, and then Stanhope and his companion halves, playing splendid football, called upon their forwards for another effort.

If Vassall had not slipped in the goal mouth after Bridges had drawn all the defence except the goal-keeper!

But the ball had bounced away just when he was in the act of trapping it. 'What a rotten funk that fellow is!' I heard someone say.

My own belief was that Vassall had slipped genuinely—there had been a slight shower directly after half-time—but the fact remained that Padmore, of whom he had shown himself all through the game to be afraid, was right on him at the time, and—well, I couldn't support my impression by much evidence, it was true.

It had been the first opportunity of the whole game. Vassall, had he only kept his feet (and head), could not have helped scoring. It was asking too much to expect another such chance to come. And the time was slipping away.

'One more, Tads'!' More frenziedly appealing than ever were the shouts.

There were only two minutes left when I glanced at my watch. Tads, next to me, was fidgeting. What a lot that goal which still eluded our forwards represented!

'Good man, Geekie!'

It was an hysterical shout. Looking up, I saw the long-legged winger making another of his fire-engine rushes down the touch-line.

He had beaten his half, but Bevan, the left-back, blocked the way to further progress.

'Centre, man!' shrieked the supporters of Tads'.

Geekie promptly acted on the instruction. The ball came across waist-high—too high for any of the inside men to gather it with comfort and without valuable time being wasted, I thought.

A fellow with dark, smooth hair, came sprinting. He met the centre with his chest, arms held high above his head, trapped the ball as it came to earth, and, in what seemed the same action, shot.

Scarcely anyone was able to follow the flight of the ball. Garside, Lorimer's goalkeeper, afterwards confessed that he did not see it himself.

But when he heard the kids at the back of him going stark, raving mad, he turned casually to inquire what the row was about.

And there was the ball resting at the back of the net!

'Just the sort of finish I expected,' said a voice which, once heard, was never forgotten. 'Centre by Geekie—goal by Vassall; it's practice does it!' went on McPhail; 'well, we've beaten Lorimer's, anyway!'

Yes, it was Vassall who had scored—in the last minute.

HE MET THE CENTRE WITH HIS CHEST

CHAPTER XI

The Secret

'Clear out for a bit,' said Stanhope, and McPhail, very unwillingly as I could see, left the study.

'I'm going to talk about Vassall—and whenever I'm talking about Vassall—whenever I *think* about him, I was going to say—I feel that that kid's eyes are boring into my head from the back! Uncanny sensation!'

The Footer Captain poured out tea and passed cakes.

'Wire in, gents,' he said; 'and when you've fed we'll have a pow-wow.'

Coming off the field, after the match with Lorimer's, Stanhope had caught hold of my arm.

'Come to tea, Dot-and-Carry,' he said; 'I want to have a jaw with you.' I met Jenkins and Bridges on the mat, and we all went in together. McPhail, pop-eyed and humming gaily to himself, was making tea.

'Well, gents, we've beaten Lorimer's,' said the skipper, when we had all finished; 'we've won our first match—and I don't know whether to be glad or sorry!'

I have already said that Jenkins was rather obtuse. Good chap, but, as Stanhope once said, he seemed to regard his head as being merely something to hang his cap on.

'I should think you ought to be glad, Skipper,' he said; 'of course, it was a near thing, but—'

Stanhope mournfully shook his head.

'It's no use, Jenks; you'll never qualify as a thinker,' he said. 'Watney, you know what I am driving at, surely?'

'I think I've got an idea.'

'Tell 'em, then!'

'What the skipper means when he said that he didn't know whether to be glad or sorry that we had beaten Lorimer's was that the scoring of that goal—a wonderful goal it was, too—by Vassall, places him in a quandary—'

'Absolutely correct, Dot-and-Carry! *Now* you can see it for yourselves?' addressing Jenkins and Bridges. 'The problem I shall have to solve is whether to continue to play at centre a fellow who funks and gets the team a beast of a name, but who can shoot like an archangel. By Jingo!' went on Stanhope, 'that goal this afternoon was one of the finest that has ever been scored at Repington!'

'A beauty!' said Jenkins.

'Garside admitted he never saw it until he turned round!' supported Bridges. 'But the chap *does* funk, Skipper—he almost ran away from comrade Padmore!'

'Exactly! You can see what I mean, can't you now? On the one hand we can't very well play the fellow again—he's a disgrace to himself as well as to the team —and yet that goal—'

'He's a wonder at trapping—and he would be at dribbling if he only gave himself the chance—oh, come in!' The first words were Bridges', the last three the skipper's.

'Hope I don't intrude, but I rather wanted to see you, Stan.'

It was Manners, the School Football Captain—the best right half-back that Repington had had for many years, to whom his team and footer generally were almost a religion. Manners played for School House, but was held in homage by the whole shop. Stanhope, proud as Lucifer to anyone else (outside his particular cronies) would have slaved for Manners.

'We'll buzz off,' said Bridges, getting up.

'Not at all—if you do, I shall go!' said Manners. 'What I have to say interests all of you.'

This being a subtle hint that Jenkins as well as Bridges and Stanhope were "possibles" for school colours that term, a quick flush of pleasure stained the cheeks of both Bridges and Jenkins. Both mumbled something unintelligible, and sat down again.

'I watched the game this afternoon,' announced Manners, 'that fellow who scored, Stanhope—isn't his name Vassall?'

'Yes,' confessed Tads' skipper, and then apologetically almost: 'I had to play him; Hastings was simply awful against Dormer's, and there was no one else.'

'We must cure him of that funking,' said Manners, crossing his legs.

'We?' said Stanhope, starting up.

Manners spoke with great deliberation.

'At present, of course, he's impossible,' he said, 'but, all the same, that chap is the finest school centre-forward in the making that I've seen since I've been here. He's got everything! That is, if you overlook his funking. Why, you've only got to see him touch a ball to know he's a player! And that goal this afternoon proved him to be perhaps the best shot in the place. I don't want what I have said to go out of this room—except among yourselves, of course—but I'm looking to you, Stanhope, to cure Vassall of habit of funking. When you do I shall give him a trial for the shop.'

'My saintly aunt!' commented Stanhope, when the school captain had gone; 'who would have thought it? But Manners is a very level-headed cove; knows what he's about generally. Of course, the chap can shoot.'

I left them still discussing the situation, and hobbled off. Like the Big Three, I was occupied with the Vassall question—so occupied that I wanted to be by myself to try to think out some solution. I might have conferred with McPhail if I could have seen him. As was, I went to my study and shut myself in.

What Manners had said was undoubtedly true: eliminate the funking, and the shop had in Vassall a potential centre-forward of great possibilities. And Repington, like Tads' House, badly wanted a centre-forward. Gilligan, that great man, had gone on to Oxford, where he was certain of his Blue, and no one as yet in the different house matches had shown any pretensions towards filling his place.

I liked Vassall, or perhaps I should not have used up so much time thinking about his affairs. I saw him—as Tads evidently saw him—as a victim of some influence which, although it caused him to be maligned and slandered, was utterly beyond his power to control.

Somehow the earliest recollections of the boy returned to me! I saw him in the train, flushing scarlet when he explained that he had never played football—and yet after two appearances in the field, Manners spoke of him as a "possible" for school colours!

But—of course, I recollected now—his father was the great Vassall! The latter must have handed down as an hereditary gift the ability to play. Vassall had the instinct.

Suddenly I was filled with the desire to know something of Vassall's splendid father. Being an old Rep —and such an illustrious one—there might be something about him in the school library.

Once in that great room, smelling faintly of musty leather, I became excited. I was like a man nearing a quest on which he had set his heart.

There were many sporting volumes—time passed—I looked through them all. At last I found what I wanted. As I read, understanding came. I guessed at the shadow which was in Vassall's life. Such a thing might well be a dominating influence. If my surmise was correct, he deserved the highest praise instead of blame.

Should I tell about my discovery? It was a matter of the gravest concern. Eventually I was forced to the conclusion that I must remain silent. If it got about the school it might cause Vassall himself very deep pain. And that would be deplorable: instead of doing Vassall some good, as was my earnest wish, I should be doing him harm. The morbid interest which would gather round him would be intolerable.

But, as I left the library, my respect for the fellow known as the funk-shy increased ten-fold.

CHAPTER XII

An Appeal

On the eve of the opening school match of season—the home fixture with Westhaven—tremendous excitement was caused by the Head's announcement that Gilbert Laidlay, the famous Corinthian, was to pay a visit to his old school in order to watch the match.

It was generally understood that Tads was responsible for the invitation. Laidlay would stay him: consequently we of Tads' House regarded the visit with special significance.

Everyone who knows anything about amateur association football of the highest class will be familiar with the career of Gilbert Laidlay. Although now past the usual playing age—he must have been at least 36 —he still turned out for the Corinthians whenever required. A sportsman in the widest sense, he had not been above playing with professionals for a professional team from time to time, and the great crowds which followed the English League team hailed him as a god. From his schooldays at Repington, where he had learnt the game, he had always been a "Star". To such a man Repington took off its cap.

He arrived, as I have said, on the eve of the Westhaven match, and— no doubt Tads, who stood high in the Head's favour, had something to do with it—came into Big Hall, where the whole school was gathered. The Head, looking more human than I had ever seen him, beamed and smiled.

'Mr. Laidlay has kindly consented to say a few words to you,' he said. 'I believe you will be interested in what he has to tell you.'

Interested! To hear a man who had played five times against Scotland as a centre-half! Besides, Laidlay looked the sportsman we knew him to be.

'I'm not much use at speeches, you fellows,' he started, with a grin that warmed us to him at once, 'but, being able to accept my dear old friend Tads' '—how the cheers broke out at the well-known abbreviation! — 'most kind invitation, I thought I would like to have a little pow-wow with you!' (Cheers again.)

'As a matter of fact, I am down here on a sort of mission—yes, I suppose it could be called a mission. The Old Reps have sent me.'

There was a general craning forward at that, for the Old Boys' Society was always demonstrating its practical love for the school. But what Gilbert Laidlay went on to say surpassed in interest any conjecture that might have been made previously.

'It's to do with your football,' he said; 'the Old Reps, through the President, Sir Arthur Lawless, has arranged to present each year a cup—it's made of silver and is rather a handsome affair—for the cock house at footer. There will be a space available on which all the names of the winning team can be engraved.'

Led by Manners, the school burst into cheers. These only died down when Laidlay held up his hand.

'And now I want to talk to you fellows quite seriously,' he said. 'Repington, as you know, is one of the few remaining public schools that play soccer.

I am not going to try to differentiate between the relative merits of Rugby and Association. Both are jolly fine sports—but we of Repington naturally think that we play the better game. That, however, is only a matter of opinion. But, playing soccer, we owe it a duty.

'Amateur football is rather at a low ebb in England at the present time. I mean the class of football which fellows of your type hope to play after you leave school. The Corinthians'—here he had to stop to allow the frantic cheering to spend its force— 'perhaps the finest club of amateurs that the world has ever known, are not the power they once were. You all, I feel sure followed our fortunes in the Association Cup last year, felt elated when we beat Blacktown, and sympathized when we lost so heavily —and deservedly, let me add—to Middleham Albion.[2]

'We, of the Corinthians, were glad to know that you, as well as the fellows of the other public schools who have remained true to soccer, were wishing us well. In return, we want you to know that, to all those who are good enough, we extend a hearty welcome to become playing members after you leave Repington.' (Cheers.)

'It may seem an unwarranted impertinence on my part perhaps' — cries of "No! No!"— 'if I appeal to you to maintain the standard of your play at its highest possible pitch. We of the Old Rep Society want not only to do well now, but to continue to do well after you leave. If the Corinthians are ever to be the playing force they once were—and that must be the fervent desire of every follower of amateur football in the

---

[2] This is a reference to the 1924 FA Cup when Corinthian FC were give a free entry into the first round where they beat Blackburn Rovers 1-0 before going onto lose 5-0 to West Brom in the second round.

country—it is essential that the club should be able to call upon recruits of the highest class.

'You of Repington have a sporting tradition to which you must try to live up,' he continued; 'those who are able to enter either your house team, or, greater honour, are privileged to gain your school colours, must always have a mental goal. Remember that by your football skill you can make it possible to help fulfil that tradition. And if you do your best, some of you will have the tremendous honour and privilege of wearing one day the colours of Corinth!' Tremendous cheering again stopped the speaker.

'Because you form part of what is comparatively a small number—most of the public schools playing Rugby—your responsibility, if I may use the word, for maintaining the standard of amateur football is the greater,' continued Laidlay. 'I hate talking to anyone about their responsibilities—that is a matter for the individual—but I am sure that you will all do the best you can.'

The meeting broke up after Manners had voiced the thanks of the school for the "ripping speech" of the visitor, but nothing else was talked about for the rest of the evening.

To me the magic quest was hopeless, of course—with my club-foot how superfluous I should have lagged upon that wonderful stage!—but many others must have seen visions in their dreams that night.

CHAPTER XIII

Vassall Looks On

Whilst all were stirred, no one in Repington listened more intently to the speech made by the famous Corinthian player than David Vassall. The words moved him so much that he had a difficulty in not crying out. It seemed that Gilbert Laidlay looked straight at him all the time he was speaking, and that he addressed his remarks directly to him.

'You . . . have a sporting tradition to which must try to live up!'

Could any other words that Laidlay might I used have given him a deeper thrust? He, the funk-shy, the Ishmael of the school which, years back had rung with the heroic deeds of his own father!

He wanted to live up to his tradition; wanted to do so with all the power that was in him. It was a fever in his blood. But that grim, mysterious dread, which had blighted his life ever since he had been at Repington, returned. Even in that moment of passionate resolution it mocked him, and told him that all his hopes were fruitless—that always It would hold him in Its merciless grip.

No one could help him—that was the terrible part of it. McPhail had tried; he had thought that staunch ally had succeeded—but directly he had stood on the field, and the game was on, the old nameless fear returned. There seemed no hope. It was ghastly.

Half an hour before the match with Westhaven started, McPhail hunted him up. 'Watney wants you to join us, Vassall,' he said.

McPhail made no comment on the other looking so downcast; disappointed as he had been in seeing Vassall give a second display of funking, he realized that the regeneration of spirit he had determined to effect could not be brought about in a week. And he had the consolation of knowing that the whole school was still talking about the wonderful goal with which Vassall had brought victory to Tads' against Lorimer's.

Watney was very decent—but then Watney always was decent to him. And Watney said an astonishing thing.[3]

'Perhaps in the next match you'll be playing, Vassall!'

He felt a hot wave go through him. This was not a light or jesting remark: Watney seemed perfectly serious. And Watney was the close friend of Stanhope, the Tads' skipper, and of practically every important fellow in the school, including Manners.

Yet Watney could scarcely have meant what he had said after all, Vassall decided; he had funked badly in his second game—and they would never risk the awful disgrace of playing a funk-shy for the school. Such a thought was inconceivable, absurd, preposterous.

Yet—the realization came instinctively—he felt that his right place was in the school eleven, leading the attack. As he stood there, watching the rival teams fraternizing before the kick-off, his spirit was on that field of play even if his body remained on the touch-line.

This was not conceit—goodness knew he had nothing about which to be conceited; it was a deep-rooted conviction. He could not have hoped to explain it. But it was a firm, unalterable consciousness, all the same.

'Manners's won the toss!' said McPhail.

All around Vassall the crowd shook with excitement. The dearest hopes these fellows had were centred in the Repington team. To them the selected players were heroes—legendary heroes almost—battling for the honour of the school, the most precious thing they knew.

Tremendous thought! If only he could harness his will sufficiently to do himself justice. But he was held a prisoner by something which was stronger than himself.

He shook himself sufficiently free of his morbid thoughts to concentrate upon the game. From all sides came snatches of information about the Westhaven team—what men were reputed to be strong, and which positions were said to be weakish. Anticipated delight was expressed at the forthcoming duel between the flying outside-left of the visitors—Morton—and Manners, the school skipper, at right-half.

'Everything will depend upon how Parkinson shapes,' Vassall heard a boy on his right say profoundly: 'he's not much good—but he's the best we've got!'

Fresh torment rent Vassall. If only he could shake off his chains, release himself from his bondage!

---

[3] A curious thing happens here in the writing. The point of view seems to switch briefly to that of Vassall for the next page or two before switching back to that of the narrator Watney.

66

But now the match had started to the accompaniment of frantic cheering from both crowded touch-lines. As excited as any of the youngsters round him, Gilbert Laidlay, the famous Corinthian, could be seen following the play with absorbed attention.

'Shoot, man!' rose the strangled cry.

But the glorious opening was wasted. From Manners, the right-half, to Laurie, the outside-right, the ball had gone. The winger had side-stepped his half, then, finding he could not round the Westhaven back, he glided a pass inside. Morris had drawn the back before pushing forward to Parkinson, who was well onside.

Had the heavily-built Repington centre been sufficiently alert he would have seized on that chance as eagerly as a hungry dog seizes a bone. There was a clear course before him—all that was required was a sprint—that and a sure foot and a clear head.

But Parkinson had not the required anticipation. Morris's brain had worked too quickly for him: he was not "up with the ball." Urged on by the cries of the crowd, he dashed forward at last, but he was too late: a Westhaven defender rushed back and booted the ball well down the field.

'No head,' commented McPhail. Vassall saw Watney nod. He, of course, said nothing.

But he knew that if he had been playing in Parkinson's place he would have anticipated that clever pass of Morris's, and would have been in position to receive it. That was if the nameless dread had not gripped him before. From the moment that Manners had first touched the ball the play had revealed itself to him as a game of chess. He saw the moves ahead.

So it was throughout the match. He might not have been able to do it himself because of his handicap of fear, but he knew exactly what Parkinson *should* have done. Many times, in Vassall's view, Repington might have scored if only Parkinson had not done the painfully obvious thing—or, rather, attempted to do it. There was that palpitating moment, for instance, when, getting clear away, the burly Repington centre-forward attempted to force a passage single-handed. If he had passed to Bridges before he was tackled by the rival right-back, "Bumper" could have drawn the defender and left him in possession again, undisputed master the situation, with only the goalkeeper to beat. As was, with Bridges running alongside, clapping his hands in frantic appeal, Parkinson attempted to do the impossible—the painfully obvious I have written above, but then, to fellows like Parkinson—all grit and not much brain—the impossible always seems to the obvious.

Of course he did not get through. When the Westhaven right-back came to the tackle, Parkinson, caught on one foot, reeled, just managed to secure the ball again, but only to lose it to the back who hoofed clear of his lines.

The match was drawn 1-1, but it was Morris, the inside-right, who got the Repington goal, not Parkinson. The latter, good, honest plodder, and plucky as they make them, was simply not up to the job. He disorganized the line instead of welding it. An individualist, he could not make it blend.

And, in consequence, Repington had to be content with a draw.

'You *must* get that centre-forward, Tads.' Gilbert Laidlay, accepting a second cup of tea, almost snapped the words. He was bitterly disappointed that he hadn't been a sufficiently good mascot to bring victory to Repington that afternoon. The play of the school team on the whole had been quite good, and with a decent centre-forward they could scarcely have helped winning by a respectable margin.

'We have him—at least I believe we have!' Tads replied enigmatically.

Laidlay stared.

'Is he sick?' he inquired, ignoring the second part of the house-master's reply.

Tads continued to be enigmatical.

'Yes—but not of the body,' he said. 'Hullo! was that a knock?'

'I believe it was.' Laidlay's face expressed his bewilderment at the other's curious manner.

Tads went to the door, opened it, said, 'Hullo, Vassall,' held a conversation, and then returned, ushering in a boy who looked very confused.

'This chap's name is Vassall,' Tads told Laidlay; 'he wants to speak to you privately, he says.'

His confusion becoming more apparent every moment, the boy waited until the house-master had left the room.

Then:

'I hope you won't think it an awful cheek, sir.'

'Cheek! Not at all! Very pleased; and I've just finished tea, too—but —well, couldn't Mr. Tadburn have heard?'

The boy reddened again.

'You can tell him afterwards if you care, sir. I scarcely liked to myself —although he knows it already.'

Gilbert Laidlay lit the one cigarette he allowed himself after each meal. He felt as puzzled over the boy's remark as he had been with the house-master's baffling statements.

'Well, fire away,' he said; 'anything I can do to help you I will. Is it anything to do with football? Sit down though first, won't you?'

'You will think me an ass, sir—but I've got to tell you from the beginning… This is my first term at Repington.'

'First term, eh! Got your place in the house team yet? By Jove! Vassall!—are you any relation of Harry Vassall who played for us—the Corinthians. I mean, of course—years ago? He was at Repington, of course.'

'Harry Vassall was my father, sir;' the youngster hung his head.

Gilbert Laidlay frowned. Harry Vassall was a father of whom any boy should have been proud—but perhaps the kid was ashamed of himself.

'What's the trouble, Vassall? Your father was great friend of mine before he—I mean, years ago. I admired him tremendously. I shall be only too pleased to do anything to help his son. You can speak to me quite frankly for it will not go further.'

The boy appeared to rally himself. 'I told you, sir, that this is my first term at Repington. I had been to a prep school before. I was supposed to be delicate—but that was all rot, of course. And I had never played football.'

'Never played football! You, a Vassall! In Heaven's name, why?'

'Do you mind if I don't answer that question, It's awfully decent of you to listen—'

'If you feel you can't tell me I shan't press of course. Carry on.'

'Just after I came here I played in a trial match for the house. I did badly—I—I funked, sir! Horribly! I let the house down.'

Laidlay's comment was surprisedly gentle.

'That was bad, of course,' he said, 'but you're not the first fellow who's funked at footer, and you certainly won't be the last.'

If he meant this for encouragement, it had its effect, for the boy began to speak with greater freedom.

'I hated myself. It's most awfully difficult to try to explain—but I couldn't help funking. Something seemed to have hold of me. I ought not to have played at all, perhaps. I had a rotten time. I deserved it—I know that.'

Laidlay nodded again. The kid was frank, anyhow. He did not attempt to make any excuses.

'Yes, I can understand that.'

'The curious thing was, sir, that I felt I could play football—I mean I found I was able to trap the ball fairly well and shoot, although I had never done anything at it before. That—you won't think I am putting on side, sir—seemed to come naturally.'

'Your father was the greatest centre-forward of his day—and they played wonderful football at that time,' said the Corinthian. 'That explains it, no doubt.'

'There is an awfully good chap here named McPhail,' continued Vassall. 'He has been taking me out, giving me private practice. I thought I had got better, and I went to Stanhope, the House Captain, and asked him to play me again. He did—but I still funked, sir—'

The Corinthian flung the cigarette which he had not finished into the fire.

'Do you know *why* you funk?' he asked.

'I seem to be afraid of getting hurt, sir.' The reply was hesitant, but plainly spoken all the same. 'But I am not afraid in other ways—when I am boxing.'

'You box?'

'Yes, sir. That was another of McPhail's ideas. He didn't say so, but I knew he thought I might cure funking at football by going in for boxing. But it didn't cure me.'

'Your friend McPhail seems to be a bright lad,' commented Laidlay. 'Of course, you want to be cured?'

'I'd give anything to be cured, sir. I felt it horribly before, but what you said last night made it worse. I want to get into the school team. And I feel I've let my father down; he would have hated the thought of my funking.

The Corinthian put his hand on the boy's shoulder. This straightforward confession had touched him deeply. He had liked the boy on sight—and liked him still more for the pluck he had shown in coming to him. Not many would have done that.

'It may interest you to know, Vassall, that when I first played football I was a funk-shy myself,' he said.

'*You*, sir!'

'Yes. It did not last very long. Like yourself, I was tremendously keen to get into the Repington team. I knew it was hopeless, however, so long as I funked. Consequently I reasoned the thing out with myself: I realized that it was a question of my mind rather than of my body. If I could control my mind, I knew I should be all right. That is the advice I give you, Vassall. You may find it difficult to follow out, but you are up against a difficult problem. Do you mind if I have a word with Tads—Mr. Tadburn—about this? You know he is a good sportsman.'

'No, I do not mind, sir. Mr. Tadburn has been awfully decent about it to me; some masters would have ragged me frightfully, I expect.'

'Not the decent sort, Vassall. But he will appreciate what I shall tell him, I know, and when you get downcast you can remember, if you like, that once I was like you are now. What I did, you can do, can't you?'

'I am going to have another jolly good try, sir!'

'Good luck to you!' said Gilbert Laidlay, and held out his hand.

CHAPTER XIV

McPhail gets the Goat

A cheque had come that morning, and McPhail was boiling over. The red-headed one was generally irrepressible, but his state was always worse when he was in funds. And he had been "Hearts of Oak" for over a week prior to the arrival of the magic envelope.

When McPhail had money he wanted to buy something. That was what money was for. The only question was what he should buy.

He had not long to wait for an idea: 'I'll get a mascot for the house team,' he told Vassall and Geekie, who formed his audience, 'a goat, for preference.'

'A mascot?' said Vassall.

'A goat?' squeaked Geekie.

'Yes—a goat,' McPhail assured them; 'I got the notion from a yarn I've just read, *McPhee*[4] it's called, and it's all about a professional football team that couldn't do right until the trainer bought a goat for a mascot. After that—well, the team won the English Cup that year! Now, no more questions, you fellows, until we've bought the blighted thing!'

Argument, in such a case, was obviously merely wasted breath, and Vassall and Geekie fell in one on each side of McPhail and walked into the town.

Standing at the corner the High Street was an impressive policeman—a veritable monument of humanity.

McPhail tapped him on the elbow—he couldn't reach much higher.

'Tell me, officer, where is the best place to buy a goat?'

The monumental one, roused from his brooding reverie, gloomed down upon his interrogator.

'Now then, young gen'l'man, none of yer he rumbled slowly.

'Larks be hanged!' replied McPhail. 'I'm not referring to birds—I want a goat. Surely you know what a goat is, officer? It stands on four legs, and smells a bit.'

---

[4] See *The Great Game/McPhee* by Sydney Horler, also released by 1889 Books.

'I ain't 'ere to be made a fool of!' came the indignant reply.

'Officer, you do me and my friends an injustice!' McPhail bowed, hand on heart. 'We are really in need of a goat—honestly, I'm not pulling your leg my dear fellow—and when we saw your kindly face standing there—I mean your feet were standing there: please don't misunderstand me again—we said: "Let us ask this nice, kind-looking policeman where we can go and buy a goat." And so here we are.'

Into the massive countenance of the law's limb crept a dull tinge of red.

'Go up to Jacob's place,' he said; 'you'll find lot of other monkeys there.'

McPhail looked pained. Then he turned to his companions.

'That is a joke,' he told them; 'we must laugh. And he proceeded to do so in such a strident note that practically all the traffic stopped.

Stopping only through want of breath, he finally "passed along," proceeding straight to a mean-looking street, from one of whose shop-fronts a sign jutted out:

ANIMALS BOUGHT AND SOLD.

'Did you know the way all along?' demanded Geekie.

'Of course! But I am naturally of a friendly disposition. I like to mix with my fellow creatures. That was why I asked that copper. Besides, one of the curses under which modern civilization groans is policemen sleeping on their beat.'

Mr. Jacobs proved to be a mild-looking gentleman, who looked not unlike a goat himself.

'Yes,' he confessed, 'I 'ave sich an animal. But goats is dear this year.'

'They're generally a bit high,' replied McPhail to Mr. Jacobs's obvious bewilderment and his companions' secret amusement; 'but lead him on, Macduff!'

'You ain't 'avin' a game with me, young gen'l'man, I 'ope,' said Mr. Jacobs with the air of one who has lost his early trust in mankind.

'My dear fellow!' protested McPhail; 'not at all! not at all! We've all been most respectably brought up, Mr. Jacobs. But a policeman we asked said that your real name was Macduff!'

'He's a liar!' declared the animal dealer; 'Jacobs is me name and it was the name of me father afore me.'

'And such is modern education!' sighed McPhail, as the indignant Mr. Jacobs led the way through the shop out into a back-yard that was suffering from extreme melancholia.

Here, tethered to a stake in the ground, was something on four legs that looked like a portrait of one of the early Assyrian kings. Mr. Jacobs declared it to be the goat.

'Wants a good blow-out—by the way, what do feed him on?' inquired McPhail.

'That ought not to be beyond our capacity,' he commented, when told.

Vassall remained silent because his astonishment had smitten him dumb, but Geekie advanced cautiously to inspect the proposed mascot.

He retired precipitously. Perhaps the goat did not care for the shape of Geekie's spectacles, or something, but, making an almost human cry, he hurled himself forward. Geekie jumped into the sky for safety.

That decided McPhail.

'He's got spirit, if he hasn't got much else,' told Mr. Jacobs; 'I'll buy him.'

'But I say, Mac, he's a man-eater!' declared Geekie, still shaking with fright.

'Then he won't touch you, Geek, old son,' replied McPhail reassuringly; 'that was only his sense of humour just now—you mustn't be misled.'

The quaint old town which slumbered restfully at the base of the hill on which Repington was perched, awoke to active life when it saw three boys, wearing the well-known school cap, marching down the High Street. The smallest youth, whose red hair was noticeable, held in his hand a rope. At the other end of the rope was a goat, which had every appearance of having lived a life of singular sinfulness. Every now and then the goat would stop to smile—or so it would seem—at the passers-by. And, invariably, the passers-by shivered.

At the school gates the porter barred the way. At least he attempted to bar the way, but the goat, who apparently had his likes and dislikes strongly defined, smiled his ghastly smile. That was sufficient: the procession passed on.

Passed on to be greeted with vociferous acclamation from every living soul in Tads', the house-master himself excepted. But appended is the dialogue:

Stanhope (from a distance). What in the deuce have you got there?

McPhail (brightly). A goat. The house team wants a mascot, so I just brought this along.

Stanhope. A mascot! But where are you going to keep it?

McPhail. Oh, that's all right. I've arranged with the groundsman.

He hadn't—but he did. Inducing other people to see his point of view was one of McPhail's strongest powers.

CHAPTER XV

Tads has a Talk

McPhail was basking in the fierce white light which invariably beat about his picturesque personality whenever he indulged in a new stunt—and this goat business was a matter over which he felt he had every reason to be gratified. Nothing quite so luridly bizarre as bringing a goat into the sacred precincts of Repington, that most orthodox of public schools, had been known within the recollection of the oldest inhabitant —Gover, the groundsman, to wit. Other fellows had kept tame mice inside their desks, one had endeavoured very laudably to brighten the dull monotony of his monastic cell (study) by smuggling a grey parrot ("warranted to talk freely") —but none had gone so far as to introduce a goat into the school life. A goat! Peter McPhail, as he remembered the decidedly satanic cast of features possessed by his recent purchase, chuckled.

He kept on chuckling to himself as he recalled the look with which Gover, the groundsman, favoured him when he walked up to that ancient leading his pet by the leash.

'Whatever 'ave you got there, Mister McPhail?' inquired Gover.

'Your sight must be failing you, old fellow,' plied the Bright Light of Repington: 'can't you see it's a goat?'

'Yes—I can not only see 'um, but I can smell 'um!' was the uncompromising response: 'what I want to make so bold as to arsk is: what be you a-goin' to do with 'um? Creeturs like that ain't allowed inside the school grounds, and well you ought to know it, Mister McPhail.'

Did McPhail flinch? Did his iron resolution falter? Did that small but sturdy frame shake with qualms? Did he repent himself of the bargain he had made? Did he tremble for the consequences? Not that anyone could have noticed it.

Instead:

'Quite so, my dear Gover—but I think you will agree with me that if nobody ever did anything but what they *ought* to do this would be a pretty

74

hollow sort of show. Now, Gover, you are absolutely the only man in the wide world to whom I would trust—I mean that Stanhope and I—'

'Did Mr. Stanhope 'ave anything to do with bringing this 'eathen animal into the school?' interjected the groundsman.

McPhail stifled a smile of triumph. He knew that Stanhope, the House Footer Skipper, was a special favourite of Gover's—which was why he had brought in his name.

'Why, of course, Gover!' he said guilelessly; 'I should have told you that before—what an ass I am! You see, this 'eathen animal is going to be the merry mascot for Tads' House in footer. I suppose you know that every important football team has a mascot? Well,' without waiting for a reply, 'this is going to be *our* mascot. And Stanhope wants you to look after him.'

'Look after a blinkin' goat, Mister that isn't included in my dooties!' said the scandalized Gover.

McPhail looked grieved.

'Look here, Gover, you aren't going to let Stanhope down, are you? He told me himself just now how much he was relying on you! Surely you aren't going to let him down? Now,' pointing to a shed at the back of the pavilion, 'what could make a nicer, more refined and generally more comfortable home for a self-respecting mascot-goat than that shed? Catch hold, Gover—I know I can leave him safely in charge.'

Before the astounded—and disgusted—Gover could make any reply, he found himself standing with the leash in his hand, while the back of the boy who had bewildered him with his blarney was receding in the distance.

With the rest of the house I had heard of the arrival of the goat, and while I smiled at the fresh ingenuity shown by McPhail to relieve the tedium of Repington existence, I wondered how Tads himself would take it.

Stanhope, who related the brief bit of dialogue had had with his fag at the entrance gate, smile proudly when I put the question to him.

'I believe McPhail would convince the Old Man himself that Repington could not possibly exist without a goat on the premises if it came to the pinch. Rest assured, Watney, that the goat will remain.' Then more seriously: 'Goodness knows we want a mascot bad enough!'

With that I agreed; and word coming just then that Tads wanted to see me, I limped away.

Arrived in Tads' room, I found McPhail already there. He acknowledged my arrival with a bright nod.

Tads smiled across at me when he entered, and then addressed McPhail.

'What is this I hear about a goat, McPhail?' he inquired mildly: 'you know the rules about—er—pets!'

'Certainly, sir,' replied McPhail at once. And then to show how thoroughly he was cognizant of them—the little brute must have swotted them up in detail just before coming into the room!—he went on: 'Pets are allowed at the school under the following conditions : First, that they are of a reasonable size and suitable—er—variety, and secondly, that they are kept outside, and not allowed to prowl about inside the school premises. Is that correct, sir?'

'Perfectly correct. But you surely do not call a goat a "pet," McPhail?'

'Certainly not, sir!' was the quick answer, 'but the 'eathen animal '—to use the picturesque phraseology of Gover, in whose charge I have just placed the creature—is not a pet. He is not intended to be a pet —he is a mascot, sir! It was for the specific object of being a mascot that I bought him this afternoon. I think you will agree, sir, that the house footer team requires a mascot?'

'Er—well, that may be so, McPhail,' the master admitted. He looked across at me as much as to say: 'What can I do with a fellow like this?'

'Then the main point of discussion is finished, I respectfully submit, sir,' replied McPhail. 'As regards the good behaviour of the goat, I pledge myself to be responsible—Gover shall receive his full instructions.'

Tads bit his lip to stop a smile.

'Very well then—so long as you promise to observe strictly those conditions, McPhail, and see that the creature is kept under control at all times. Perhaps I ought not—but that will do. Clear—I want to have a word with Watney.'

'I am very much obliged, sir,' said McPhail gravely, and left the room with the demeanour of an ambassador having received a favour on behalf of his Government.

'An amazing youth, Watney—but it's not about McPhail that I wanted to talk to you—it's about Vassall.'

I nodded but said nothing, wondering what was coming next.

The house-master slumped into a chair, and lit his pipe.

'I like Vassall—and I want to help him,' Tads continued: 'this funking business of his goes deeper than mere football, although I grant you that is important enough. I can tell you in confidence that Vassall is so keen on getting rid of his weakness that he actually had a private chat about it to Gilbert Laidlay when he was here recently. Laidlay told me. That wanted a little pluck on the fellow's part, I think you will agree, Watney?'

'It certainly did, sir.'

'The human mind is a puzzling thing—and it is a problem of the mind we have to face in the case of Vassall. The question is: How can we eradicate the fear of getting hurt from Vassall's mind when he is on the football field?'

'By Jove, if it could only be done!' I said eagerly, leaning forward. 'Perhaps you know what Manners thinks about Vassall, sir?—that Vassall would be the best centre-forward the school has had for years, if he could only overcome his funking!'

'Yes, I know that—I think so myself. In fact, I am sure of it. That is one of the reasons why I am so anxious to do all I can to help.'

But after a long discussion both Tads and I were forced to the conclusion that the cure must come from the boy himself. It was a matter in which no one outside could help him.

CHAPTER XVI
The Merry, Merry Mascot

It was stated before the house team went up against Wyvern's that Vassall would not be playing. Naturally enough, after all that had gone before, it was assumed that Stanhope, in spite of the brilliant goal the funk-shy had scored against Lorimer's, had got "fed" with him and had dropped him once again.

Rumour once more lied; Vassall had sprained his ankle in jumping a hedge during a country training walk, and could only limp. It was rough luck, but he had the satisfaction of knowing that he had been down to play before he reported to the House Captain that be was not fit.

Wyvern's crowd were almost cock-a-whoop about the result, even before a ball had been kicked.

After rubbing Lorimer's nose in the dirt to the time of 2-1, there was a quiet confidence in the Tads' camp. It was felt that a revival might be coming after the disastrous start made by the team, and when the teams lined up, the whole of the house were ready to cheer.

The match will go down in Repington history on account of the concluding scene. But I am before my story.

The start was disastrous from our point of view; Withleigh, a weedy youngster, who played outside-right for Wyvern's, tricked Birtles with ridiculous ease after outpacing the Tads' left-half, and finished up by centring so precisely that the Wyvern centre-forward merely had to nod the ball into the net, our goalkeeper being powerless.

Standing by the side of Vassall, who was following the play with the keenest interest, I saw Stanhope direct a questioning look at Birtles. It was undoubtedly the latter's fault that Tads' were one down within three minutes of the start

As the play went on it was seen that Birtles was out of training; he must have been playing the fool in some way or another. Anyhow, he simply could not hold Withleigh who rounded him time after time.

'Play up, Birtles!' chanted the juniors, disgusted at the rotten show he was giving.

With a goal down, and a further reverse threatening any moment, the anxious Stanhope shifted Jenkins to the more dangerous wing of the opposition, but although this remedied one weakness, it allowed the Wyvern's outside-left, who up till now, because of the careful shepherding of Jenkins, had been comparatively innocuous, to take heart of grace and put his best leg forward.

The left wing of Wyvern's had become as difficult to hold as had the right. And all because of the extraordinary weakness of Birtles.

The hearts of the juniors must have been down in their boots when Bridges relieved the general gloom by snapping up a centre from Geekie —who proved that his form against Lorimer's was no mere flash in the pan by trotting out another amazing show—and shooting hard on the run before either of the opposing backs could close with him.

It was a rocket ball, a real dazzle drive, one of Bridges' best. It sped past the outstretched hand of the Wyvern goalkeeper while all the world —all Tads' world, that is—cheered as though it had suddenly gone mad.

The scores were equal—but with Birtles playing like a drunken fool at right-back, what might still happen?

But half-time came with the scores still level, although our goal had had some jolly narrow shaves. Only miraculous 'keeping by Merrick had managed to compensate for the continued uselessness of Birtles.

'The chap must be ill,' was the general opinion, but Tads, who had strolled up to have a word with me, looked more serious than sorry.

'He certainly doesn't look well,' he said.

The second half was a replica of the first. Our forwards could not get through the opposing defence, but there seemed every chance for Wyvern's to get through ours. Much against his own will—for he was essentially a fighting skipper—Stanhope in the last quarter of an hour gave up the idea of forcing a win, and concentrated his attentions on keeping Wyvern's out.

The minutes sped slowly. Each time Wyvern's came attacking it seemed that the inevitable must happen. And in the last five minutes it would have happened, but for what seemed at the time a miracle.

It is difficult to describe, but I must make the effort. Answering the call of their captain, Wyvern's made a final determined rush. The ball went to Withleigh, their outside-right, and he planted it into the centre again, since he knew that this was a far safer course than trying to beat Jenkins, with whom he had had many unsuccessful trials of skill.

The inside-left seized on the pass, drew the Tads' right-half and sped on.

'Stop him, Birtles! Oh, buck up, man! Play up, Birtles!'

Whether the shouts were the means of accomplishing the final discomfiture of Birtles, I do not know, but we saw him make a reckless rush at the inside-left, miss him, and fall on his hands and knees in the mud.

In the terrific excitement which prevailed no one realized the amazing occurrence which was taking place outside the playing-pitch until someone yelled: 'Look out! Look out!'

The speaker gave a mighty yell and then leapt high into the air. It was then that we saw the thoroughly surprising spectacle of an evidently overwrought and apparently angry goat charging through the dissolving ranks of spectators straight into the playing pitch.

Straight up to the prostrate form of Birtles! Whether the right-back's hindquarters were a barrier that the goat resented seeing in his path, it is difficult to tell, but what we saw was this: the goat lowering his head and butting Birtles amidships with such force that the right-back was hurled forward. In his flight he collided with Gordon, the Wyvern's inside-left who, having beaten Jenkins, had our goal completely at his mercy. At the actual moment that Birtles so unexpectedly collided with him, he was preparing to shoot, but the ball went soaring over the bar instead of under. A miracle had saved Tads'!

'Oh, dear me, that was very funny!'

I looked round, for I thought I had recognized the voice. It belonged to the Old Man himself, the Head! While the world stood agape, the Austere One had his laugh out.

Then, suddenly, as though realizing how completely and profoundly he must have fallen from the Olympian heights, he frowned.

'Watney, how did that animal enter the school grounds?' He had addressed me, I suppose, because I was the nearest senior.

I opened my mouth to mumble some sort of non-committal answer when I was forestalled.

'If you please, sir, it belongs to me! McPhail!'

'Belongs to you, McPhail?'

'Well, to be strictly accurate, sir, I should say it belongs to the house. I bought it for a mascot, sir—and,' gravely, 'on its first appearance it seems to have done its work very well.'

The Head turned away. He was choking with laughter which he was trying vainly to suppress.

'Ah, Mr. Tadburn, you will see that—that the animal is kept under proper restraint in future.'

With that he walked away. Whatever the future of the goat might be, he evidently was not in a fit state of mind to discuss the matter at that moment. So ended the match with Wyvern's.

So far as football was concerned it ended there. But that tea-time, after the goat had been securely fastened in its quarters by Gover, the groundsman, Birtles tip-toed into Stanhope's study.

McPhail, making tea, stared. The fellow looked dangerous.

'Where's Stanhope?' the visitor demanded.

'I don't know. He will be here any minute, though.'

Birtles showed his teeth in a ghastly grin. He closed the door, and advanced upon McPhail.

'He can come in if he likes, but he won't stop me from showing you that you can't make a fool of me without paying for it.'

'What's the joke?' inquired McPhail. He the fellow was in a dangerous mood, but he was not going to show fear before the brute.

'Joke!' snarled Birtles.

Any further words seemed to choke him. He rushed at McPhail and caught him by the collar. In struggling the fag upset the teapot which fell with a crash to the floor.

'Oh-h!' McPhail could not help the sob, for the other had hit him with vicious force.

Then the door burst open.

'Birtles!'

Stanhope, a stern look on his face, had caught the arm before it could descend again. 'What do you mean lamming a junior—and my fag?'

Birtles smothered an oath. 'I shouldn't advise you to butt in, Stanhope,' he snarled, 'oh, I don't forget that you're a pre, and captain of football—but all the same I repeat that. I shouldn't advise you to butt in. It might be dangerous for you. I have been waiting for the chance to teach this young cub manners for some time past—and this afternoon finished it!'

'What did he do this afternoon?' asked Stanhope, and then a remembrance came back to him and he smiled.

That smile was like a red rag flaunted in the face of a furious bull. Birtles launched a blow straight at Stanhope's face.

If the Football Captain had not ducked he might have been knocked senseless.

'That was rather a foolish thing to do, Birtles,' he said quietly; 'McPhail, just clear out for a moment, will you? Oh, no you don't,' as Birtles made a move to prevent the fag from leaving.

The door closed behind him; Birtles glared.

'It seems to me that you're taking just a little much on yourself, Stanhope. I'm hanged if I'm to put up with it much longer. If you weren't prefect—'

'Well?' inquired Stanhope coldly; 'assume for a moment that I'm not a prefect, what then?'

'I would give you a licking—that's what,' was reply.

'I see,' replied Stanhope; 'we'll come back to that a little later if you don't mind. What I want tell you now is that if you continue to slack training, as you must have been doing lately, I shall drop you from the team. You realize, I suppose, that it was   due to your rotten game that we only drew with Wyvern's to-day?'

'What do I care about your rotten team?' sneered Birtles.

'Exactly. You are cad enough not to care—and you proved it this afternoon. That is all I have to say—except that I strongly advise you not to attempt any bullying of McPhail in the future.'

Stanhope turned away in cool, but dignified, dismissal of the other, but then wheeled swiftly. He had the presentiment that Birtles would attack him behind his back.

He closed with the back before Birtles could deliver the blow which threatened, and there was an unseemly struggle for a few moments.

Then the Football Captain, wrenching himself free, said: 'I don't want to fight you, Birtles, but you force me to.'

Birtles's face glowered.

'Will you fight?—and forget that you are a prefect?' he asked.

The implication that he might take advantage of his position by reporting Birtles, should the latter lick him in the tussle, enraged Stanhope so much that he forthwith flung off his coat.

'I don't think I will answer that question, Birtles.'

The left-back, in reply, joyfully took off his own oat. The joy of smashing his clenched fist into the other's cold face!

Came a knock on the door.

'May I come in, Stanhope?'

Tads' voice!

Stanhope could not pull himself together in time to top the master from entering.

Tads took one searching glance at the two shirt-sleeved antagonists, and added: 'What's going on here?'

Stanhope coughed.

'Birtles was going to show me a new upper-cut that he has learned at boxing, sir,' he replied.

'I see.' The tone was dry. 'Well, perhaps that very interesting demonstration had better be postponed for a while.' He looked at Birtles, who took the hint and his coat, and vanished.

'You were going to fight that fellow, Stanhope?'

The Football Captain looked straight at his questioner.

'Yes, sir—I was.'

Tads' comment was characteristic.

'No doubt you had ample excuse—but, all the same, it was fortunate that I dropped in to stop it. I have an idea that we are going to have considerable trouble with Birtles in the future, and it would not do to have an open rupture between you as Footer Captain and him. You understand, Stanhope?'

'Quite, sir—and I'll try to remember it in future.'

But both knew inwardly that the fight which had been so narrowly averted was bound to take place sooner or later. There was too much undercurrent of feeling on both sides for it to be indefinitely "off;" it was merely postponed to a future date.

CHAPTER XVII

The Mystery of the Motor-bike

'I feel,' said McPhail, sniffing the air, 'that I want to look upon the world this afternoon. I want to see the earth and all the glory thereof. There isn't any football, and even if there were my soul needs a change. What about it, Vassall?'

David Vassall, who seemed to find the world a much better place than it used to be, judging by the expression he now had, smiled.

'If you like—and Tads would give us a pass to lock-up—I could hire a motor-bike and—'

'I to ride pillion like the flappers on the magazine covers?' exclaimed McPhail; 'oh, delirious joy! Hie thee unto Tads then, most Admirable of Crichtons[5], and, behold, I will come too to add my weighty arguments to the counsel!'

As it happened, it did not require McPhail's "weighty arguments" to induce Tads to give the necessary permission. 'Only be careful that you don't do any further mischief to that ankle—we shall want you in the next house match, you know, Vassall,' he added, with an emphasis that brought a flush of pleasure into the boy's face.

The village, like every other hamlet on the face of the map nowadays, had its inevitable motor and cycle garage, and it was from one of the latter that Vassall was able to borrow a fairly serviceable motor-cycle. The vintage was somewhat ancient it was true, but it seemed safe enough.

'Lo! the brave knight and his fayre lady,' said McPhail, as he got on the pillion seat.

'Of course you young gents understand that you'll be responsible for any damage that may be done to the machine?' cut in the romance-blighting voice of the garage owner.

---

[5] A, now, little-used cliché, referring to the Scot, James Crichton, who died in a street fight in Mantua in 1582 at the age of 21 having become the ultimate Renaissance man: adept in languages, the arts, sciences, music poetry, sword-fighting, horse-riding and what-not – as well as being good-looking, apparently.

'So be it!' replied McPhail, 'let her go, George!' And the voyageurs shot off in a cloud of dust and petrol fumes.

A glorious sense of freedom possessed them. They were masters of their fate and lords of their destiny until 6.30 that evening. The lure of the open road was theirs; they travelled on and on almost regardless of time and space.

It was not until Vassall glanced at his watch and how late it was that he turned the motor-cycle round.

'It's half-past four and we'd better be getting back he said to his companion.

'But what about tea?' demanded McPhail; 'we must have food to stay our stomachs. How can hope to face the arduous return journey unless we have some tea?'

'Oh, well, if you must feed,' answered Vassal patiently, and headed towards a cottage with a thatched roof standing back from the road, outside the entrance-gate of which stood a sign:

TEAS PROVIDED.

'The sign is a bit moth-eaten, but the cottage looks all right,' commented McPhail. 'I suppose it safe to leave this load of iron outside?'

'I should think so,' agreed Vassall; 'there's not much passing, and in any case who would want to pinch a thing like this?'

Their minds thus comforted, they walked up the flagged path, and McPhail knocked at the door.

'Tea?' repeated the comely old dame with the white cap and russet-apple cheeks when she heard the request: 'certainly you shall have some tea, me dears! Come along in, and I'll have it all ready for you in two shakes of a lamb's tail. Now what would you like—eggs?'

McPhail agreed that eggs were a capital suggestion.

'Toast, me dears?'

That proposition was also declared carried—as were all the other ideas that this very talented provider of teas put forward. Never was there such unanimity!

McPhail—always a good trencherman—ate steadily for twenty minutes, and then pushed plate and cup away reluctantly.

'I herewith on behalf of the nation award you the Sacred Order of the Home-made Cake,' he said to the provider of the feast.

'I do hope you have enjoyed it, me dears—and that you have had enough to eat. That'll be a shilling each, if you please.'

'A shilling!—only a shilling! Granny darling—I herewith award you with a second Sacred Order of the Home-made Cake!—if there were more women in the world like you the world would be a far better place.

85

If I wasn't so dashed old I'd—I'd kiss you on the spot!'

'I'm sure you're very welcome, me dear!' but then Vassall, thrusting half a crown into her hand left the room in order that he might have his laugh out in peace.

Joined by McPhail they strolled leisurely up to the entrance of the garden path.

'We can get home and have a bath,' he said.

McPhail coughed. 'Yes, I think we shall want one when we get back-to the shop—for it seems to me that we shall have to walk.'

'Walk?' echoed Vassall, thinking that McPhail, as usual, was joking. 'Don't be—'

And then he stopped. The motor-cycle was gone. It was not there!

'Stolen!' he gasped.

'Pinched of a truth,' agreed McPhail; 'the question is: by whom?'

'What does that matter?' Vassall felt compelled to ask. 'You go that way and I will go this. See if we can catch sight of the rotter.'

But both, when they returned panting, confessed that they had not been able to catch sight of the thief.

'A nice thing—I don't think,' said McPhail, how far is it to the shop, do you reckon?'

'A good ten miles—and we have an hour to in!'

'And I had such a tea. Oh, mother, I can't do it—not in these trousers, anyway!'

'You will have to do it!' And, as the reflection crossed his mind, making it very uneasy, 'What shall we tell the garage man?'

'Thank Heaven the thought of that greasy-looking blighter had faded from my mind—until you have so cruelly reminded me of him,' replied McPhail; 'tell him that he must collect the insurance money, I suppose. What else can we tell him?'

'He'll expect us to pay up £20 or so, I am afraid.' Vassall's tone was lugubrious; the motor-cycle had been borrowed in his name, and although he knew that McPhail would nobly stand his whack, yet the prospect of having to find £10 was even more disheartening than the ten-mile walk which stretched between them and Repington.

'There's nothing for it, I am afraid,' he told McPhail, and the other, after shuddering, stepped out by his side.

'I wonder if singing would make it appear any shorter—something bright and military about the Long, Long Trail, you know?'

Vassall briefly replied that he did not think it would —his mind was not exactly in tune with melody just then—and so the junior subsided.

They had walked a mile or so along the road, and hadn't encountered a soul when McPhail burst into an angry protest.

'This place is dead!' he said; 'where are the simple villagers with their boundless hospitality and horse-carts? Oh, to see a cart now!'

In the distance could be heard a humming noise. Pausing to listen, McPhail declared his prayer to be answered. 'Only it's better than a cart; it's a motor-car!—I say, it can't be the motor-cycle come back, I suppose. Penitent thief weeping all over the handle-bars—that sort of thing?'

'I'm afraid not—the fellow who took that motor-cycle isn't a bit penitent, I feel sure. Suppose it is a motor-car?' he added, looking at the other.

'My dear Vassall, the question is superfluous! What are the facts? The facts are (one) an approaching motor-car proceeding in the direction of the shop, and (two) two stranded and forlorn scholars anxious to return to that seat of learning. *Ergo*, as they say in the classics, I shall jolly well ask for a lift, and if they are churls enough to refuse it I shall hang on to the foot-board.'

'We shall see,' replied the more cautious Vassall.

It happened that when the car approached schoolboys, it pulled up at once. The driver, a coarse-looking, red-faced man, dressed in very loud tweeds, leaned over.

'What you two boys doin' here?'

Afraid that McPhail's irrepressible nature would lead him to say something which would give the man offence, Vassall answered.

'We came out for a ride on a motor-cycle. While we were having tea the thing was stolen, and so we started to walk back. I wonder if you would be kind enough to give us a lift—that is if you are going in the direction of Repington.'

'Jump in,' was the reply. 'I'll drive you straight to the school or near enough that it doesn't matter.' The speaker turned to Vassall, whom he evidently considered to be the more responsible person. 'Do you know a boy named Birtles?' he inquired.

'Yes,' replied Vassall, wondering what could be coming, 'I know Birtles.'

'Well, young gen'l'man, you can pay me back for taking you home by telling Master Birtles, when you meet him, that I want to see him particular, and that he had better come to see me. Can you remember that?'

'What name shall I tell him?'

'Joe Binks is me name,' answered the red-faced gentleman with emphasis; 'you'll be careful not to forget, won't you, young gen'l'man?'

'Yes, I won't forget,' replied Vassall.

"WHAT YOU TWO BOYS DOIN' HERE?"

CHAPTER XVIII

Birtles is Staggered

Vassall turned away. 'Your business isn't likely to interest me, Birtles,' he said; 'I have kept my promise to the man who was decent enough to give McPhail and myself a lift when we were stranded ten miles away from the school—that is all. Why Mr. Joe Binks should wish to see you doesn't concern me—I am merely passing on his remark to you.'

'Eugh!' grunted Birtles; 'it's just as well for you that you didn't push your nose in any further, my lad!'

Before Vassall could reply to the gratuitous insult, he had gone, slamming the door after him. But his customary swagger was absent; he looked like one who had received a nasty jar.

While Vassall was debating whether he should follow the fellow, McPhail came into the study.

'Life is getting very interesting,' remarked the visitor; 'I've just come from Stanhope—there's the beginnings of an unholy row brewing between Stanhope and Birtles. Mr. B. has chucked training and says that he won't turn out for the house team again—which will be just as well, of course, if he can't play better than he did against Wyvern's. Vassall,' breaking off and changing the subject abruptly, 'I'd give a great deal to know who stole that motor-cycle.'

'Some tramp who was tired of footing it, I expect,' replied Vassall.

'M' yes—perhaps,' said McPhail; 'anyway, I've taken certain steps this afternoon to try to have my curiosity satisfied. I've been to a private detective johnny—an old Scotland Yard man, retired on pension who lives in the village.'

'What do you expect him to find out?' inquired Vassall.

'Something that may be startling,' replied McPhail cryptically.

Vassall still kept up his boxing lessons under the tutelage of Benny Bennison, and it was after returning from the gymnasium one afternoon that he met McPhail. The latter was in a state of bubbling excitement.

'I want to have a chat with you—the "something startling" which I partly prophesied has happened!' declared Stanhope's fag.

Pressed for further information, McPhail stated that he had just received a message from the retired detective he had employed in the affair of the missing motor-bike, and that he was now on his way to the man's house.

'You had better come along with me, old horse,' he added.

There being still an hour to lock-up, Vassall agreed to this course, and within ten minutes they were sitting in a pleasantly situated room looking at the portly framed ex-crime investigator of Scotland Yard.

'I have discovered the thief of the motor-cycle, gentlemen,' announced Joseph Simpson, 'and it is because I want to know your intentions, Mr. McPhail that I sent you the message this afternoon. Of course, stealing an article of the value of a motor-cycle is a serious offence —an offence for which a person may be sent to prison—but as this thief is a school chum of yours—'

'What do you say?' demanded Vassall, scarcely able to believe his ears, but McPhail merely nodded, as though he was not at all surprised by the information, startling though it was.

'I have discovered that the person who stole this motor-cycle is a boy at Repington School,' replied the former detective deliberately. 'I will now tell you his name'—he did so, causing a gasp of astonishment to come from Vassall—'and how it was managed.'

Ten minutes later the two boys left the house. Vassall was speaking earnestly.

'If he agrees to send the bike back to the garage, we can't do anything more.'

McPhail whistled.

'You're an amazing cove, Vassall,' he replied; 'of course, I know it wouldn't be exactly cricket to get the rotter the sack—and that is what he would get if Stanhope or Tads ever got to hear about it—but at the same time, after all he has done against you—'

'I'm not going to lick him that way,' said Vassall. 'Mac, leave this to me, will you?'

'Certainly.' McPhail proved his metal by agreeing instantly.

'And you will keep this absolutely to yourself?— not say a word to anyone, not even to Stanhope?'

'Not a word—but what's the idea, Vassall? You surely aren't going to let the thing drop completely? A swine who's a low down, common thief *ought* to be chucked out—'

'That's all right. He's not going to get off scot-free. But I want to settle this job in my own way, if you don't mind.'

90

'Oh, all right. But you'll tell me about it afterwards?' It was a monstrous thing according to McPhail that the course of justice should be allowed to run on such unorthodox and undramatic lines.

'Yes—I will tell you about it—when the time comes. Don't worry.'

But McPhail, as he departed to get tea ready for Stanhope, shook his head.

Vassall, his mind in a whirl, felt he wanted solitude—and room to think. He set off on a walk round the dusk-laden, deserted playing-fields.

Fate had worked in a dramatic fashion: it had delivered his worst enemy at Repington into his hands. He had only to say a word, and the fellow who had gone out of his way to make life at Repington a hell for him would vanish, never to return. He would go, too, in shame and ignominy.

Absorbed in his thoughts, he almost stumbled in the gloom. He was near the groundsman's hut.

Suddenly he heard a riot of noise. Listening, he came to the conclusion that someone was inside ill-treating the goat which was McPhail's latest and special joy. Gover, the groundsman, had evidently left for the night, and some skunk—

He softly opened the door of the hut and stepped inside. By the light of a candle—the only illumination in the place—he saw a tall youth wielding a long pole, at the end of which was a short spike. This pole had once formed part of a cricket-practice batting net.

A tethered goat—McPhail's pet and the mascot of the house footer team—was the object of the youth's cruelty and vicious attentions. The latter consisted in pricking the goat—which, being closely tethered, was Birtles is Staggered 141 powerless—and laughing gleefully at the pain inflicted.

'Put that thing down!'

His blood at boiling-point, he rapped out the command. Vassall could see now who the tormentor was—Small, a loutish youth, big and vicious, who thought it brave and manly to scorn all games, and who had earned the contempt of all decent fellows in the house in consequence. Lately Birtles had been seen often in the company of Small, who, everyone in Tads' knew, would be expelled by the Head at the slightest further provocation.

Small, in the act of pricking the goat again—he had been too absorbed in his pleasurable task to notice that the door of the hut had opened—stared.. Then his mean eyes contracted.

'Why, it's the courageous funk-shy!' he sneered; 'what are you doing all alone out in the dark? Aren't you afraid?'

'Put down that pole, you swine!' cried Vassall, in reply. The sight of the blood-flecked side of the goat roused him to a frenzy.

'Why not come and take it from me?'

Vassall immediately accepted the challenge—to the surprise of Small evidently, for he presented the sharp spike in the other's direction, and if Vassall had not learnt his football swerve he might have received a very nasty wound.

But the next moment he had grappled with the vicious lout, and to use the picturesque phraseology of Mr. Benny Bennison, "was knocking-out of him." Vassall had not hit anyone in anger since he had taken up boxing, but now he rained blows upon the animal-torturer until Small whimpered in futile rage and pain.

Finally, with a right-handed swing, he knocked the lout reeling to the floor of the hut. Small lay still. He had had enough of goat-pricking and fighting combined for the time being.

'Get up, you swine—you can't lie there!' said Vassall, and when Small refused the pressing invitation to get up on his feet again, he caught him by the coat-collar, yanked him upwards with one mighty heave, and then hurled him outside into the darkness.

In falling Small collided with someone who was about to enter the hut. There was the sound of a smothered oath, and then a voice said: 'What the blazes do think you are playing at, Small? Is the thing loose?'

'The goat—if that is what you are referring to Birtles—is not loose,' answered Vassall, 'but all same, I shouldn't advise you to try any tactics like friend Small.'

Birtles's astonishment at hearing Vassall's voice was evidently so great that he could not find anything to say for the moment. And before he did speak another form loomed out of the darkness.

'What in the 'tarnal mischief is a-goin' on here?' inquired the voice of Gover, the groundsman.

'Something which requires your attention, Gover,' replied Vassall. 'Someone has been tormenting the goat, and it wants looking after.'

The groundsman, who loved all animals—even such a grotesque specimen as the goat which had been into his charge—dashed inside. He was heard muttering beneath his breath, and then he burst out again:

'Who did it? What 'eathen did it?'

'Look here, Gover, I didn't mean any harm. It only a joke.' Small had scrambled to his feet.

'No 'arm, you darned butcher, you! You drew blood—the poor thing is a shameful sight! If I could have my way with you I'd choke the life out of your ugly carcass. It's the 'Eadmaster who'll be 'earin' of this.'

Small, like a dog who has been whipped, slunk away.

The lock-up bell rang the next moment.

'I want to see you, Birtles, to-night—after prayers, either in your study or mine,' said Vassall; and Birtles (somewhat surprisingly) growled: 'Oh, all right—come along to me.'

But he spoke as though he had received a shock.

CHAPTER XIX

The Reason

'Well?' demanded Birtles sullenly. Two facts were plain. The first that, with all native surliness and bombast, he dreaded this talk and secondly that he was putting up the best fight in order to try to prove that he was indifferent.

'I've come to have a straight talk with you, Birtles—it's time we had one, I think. Ever since I have at Repington you have gone out of your way to be as rotten as possible to me—'

'Good Lord! You don't imagine for a moment you're the sort I should cling to, do you?'

'You're the last fellow in the world—with possible exception of Small—that I should want to have clinging to me,' was the level reply, 'but, as I have said, you have gone out of your way to be rotten. Why?'

The question came with startling swiftness.

'Why?' replied Birtles after a pause. 'Because in the first place, I hate the darned sight of you. I hate your name, too.'

'Why?' demanded Vassall with cold logic again. 'I don't pretend to be a matinee idol, and my name is as good as yours, if it comes to that.'

'Your mother's an arrant snob,' countered Birtles.

The other's face became white.

'This is strictly an affair between our two selves, Birtles—we will leave my mother out of it, if you please. Have you any other reasons why you should try to be a cad towards me?'

'Hang it, aren't you the most disliked fellow in the house? Why pitch on me in particular? Everyone in Tads' is down on you! We don't want a funk in the house, and it's time you realized the fact.'

'Part of that statement is untrue—and you know it's untrue. Everyone in Tads' isn't down on me. Even if I have funked at football, I have some good friends.'

'Stanhope!' sneered Birtles, 'a fellow who's keeping out of my way these days because he knows what's coming to him if he doesn't! And

McPhail—a fag! Geekie, also, a fool—a fine choice of friends!'

'Very well, we won't discuss that particular side of the question. But either McPhail or Geekie is a jolly sight better friend than a fellow like Small. However, that isn't the question I want to ask you—'

'You seem to be pretty keen on asking questions,' sneered Birtles.

'Yes, I have a particular reason in asking this one.'

Birtles tried to look unconcerned—but didn't quite succeed.

'What is it?'

'Where is the motor-cycle which you stole on Tuesday afternoon?'

Birtles sprang to his feet, his face distorted.

'You had better be careful what you are saying!' he spluttered, 'or I'll smash your face in!'

'My face can take care of itself—and you had better answer my question. What have you done with the motor-cycle you stole on Tuesday afternoon?'

Birtles's rage died out of his face. He slumped back into his chair.

'Perhaps I had better explain the position a little more fully,' said Vassall. 'On Tuesday afternoon I hired a motor-cycle at Browning's shop in Market Place. McPhail and I went for a ride in country. We had tea at a cottage at a place Little Ridings, or some such name as that, about ten miles out.

'We thought an hour would be ample time which to get back before lock-up at half-past and so it would have been if, when we came out of the cottage where we had had tea, we hadn't discovered that someone had removed the motor-bike. As the bike didn't belong to me I was naturally anxious about it. As a matter of fact a private detective was consulted—and he gave us certain information this afternoon.'

'Us—who do you mean—"us"?' snapped Birtles. He no longer made any passionate disclaimers.

'McPhail and myself. McPhail knew this private detective.'

'And what did this big-footed policeman tell you?'

In reply, Vassall spoke lucidly, concisely, slowly, for perhaps five minutes. At the end of time he looked straight into the ashen face of Birtles.

'Why you did it, I don't want to know,' he said, 'and so far as I am concerned, if you take the bike back to Browning's place the matter will be dropped. You can rely upon McPhail not saying anything, and the detective fellow has now finished with it.'

Birtles swallowed something.

'The facts are dead against me,' he replied. 'I admit I took the bike, but I didn't mean to steal it. But I'm not going into that now; I don't want to give you any more cause for gloating satisfaction.'

'If I wanted gloating satisfaction I should have gone to Tads and not come to you,' he was told; 'even you will admit that I have been given cause enough.'

'I took the bike even if I didn't intend to sneak it—that's enough for you to go to the Head with.'

'I'm not going to the Head—not even to Tads,' was the reply.

Birtles stared.

'Why not? I was a fool to give you any chance—but I hated you—hate you now more than ever! But now that I've given you the chance to get me the sack, why aren't you going to the Head, pray?'

'Because I'm going to lick you in another way than that, Birtles! *That* is when I shall get my "gloating satisfaction," as you have called it.'

Before the other could reply, he had left the room.

All unaware of the drama that had taken place in Birtles's study the night before, Repington woke the next morning to find the stage set for a resounding scandal.

Rumour was busy from the earliest moment. The evil, but sensational, news might have travelled on wings through the night. The yarn had it that Small ("that swine! well, it won't be much loss") was to be expelled. It was all Vassall's—yes, Vassall, the house football funk-shy's—doing. He had gone to Tads with some yarn, and Tads had gone straight off to the Head. What in the deuce could it have been? What had the fellow done?

The school was not kept long in suspense. The command went round that all houses were to assemble at once in Big Hall.

A morbid thrill passed through almost everyone who heard it. That meant a public expulsion. What *had* the fellow done?

It was an awful moment, when, with the school assembled, and the wretched Small, standing in isolated disgrace, the Headmaster of Repington commenced his speech.

'I have called you together this morning to witness me perform a most unpleasant but a necessary and I firmly believe a just duty.' The opening, sonorous words, laden with a sad gravity, rang out, sending little nervous tremors through the listeners.

'This boy here,' he indicated the shivering Small, 'has been found guilty of a particularly abominable act. He was seen by another boy in Mr. Tadburn's House torturing—cruelly torturing—a helpless animal last night. His conduct was so malicious and cruel that I have been forced to come to the conclusions that Small, about whose previous behaviour in certain grave matters I have long had my most earnest doubts, is no longer a fit person to remain at Repington. He will consequently be expelled, and will leave the school almost immediately. It may seem a cruel sentence that I have imposed, but I want you all to remember and realize,' here the voice took on an even more ringing note, 'that the honour of Repington will always be considered by me above the private feelings of any individual. And I construe it as my bounden duty to send from us anyone whose conduct is likely to disgrace the name of this school, or is likely to contaminate the behaviour of any of the guilty person's associates. I want this scene to sink deeply into the minds and memories of everyone here. That is all; you will dismiss!'

So passed Small—a human blot on the life of a great school. I do not believe that it was solely on account of the specified offence of cruelty to the goat that the Head expelled him; what I do believe is that various evidence of a particularly obnoxious and unpleasant nature had been accumulating against Small for some time, and that the Head utilized the opportunity which had been given him.

Naturally discussion raged as to the ethical part which Vassall had played in the matter. The majority, I was glad to know, ruled in Vassall's favour. It was not until after the storm had died down that the school learned it was Gover, the groundsman, who had complained directly to the Head, and that the only part Vassall played in the unsavoury episode was to give evidence when the Head called upon him to do so. Of course, he had to do that.

CHAPTER XX

Vassal "Makes Up"

It was always a great occasion at the shop when the Old Reps brought down a team to play the school. Not only was the play of the visitors generally of a high class (some were men of Corinth, don't forget), but the visit served as a jollification all round. These re-unions were splendid affairs.

Tads went himself to the station with Manners, the school skipper, Stanhope, and a few others to welcome the Old Reps' team. The first face that poked itself out of the third-class railway carriage belonged to Gilbert Laidlay.

He was greeted with a ring of welcoming faces. But his own was somewhat cloudy.

'How are you all?' he said, and then: 'I say Manners, you'll have to lend us a forward—Thurston wired this morning to say he couldn't get away and we were too late to bring anyone else.'

'Oh, rotten luck!' said the skipper of Repington, 'but of course we will help you to make up. You can have whom you like—outside the team. Where did Thurston play?'

'Centre-forward.'

Tads' face showed excitement.

'We can fix it all right, Laidlay,' he remarked; 'if you'll excuse me now I'll cut back to the school.' He turned to Manners: 'I hope we shall agree about the boy who plays, Manners.'

The skipper, who had absolute faith in Tads, and only wished that he belonged to his house, smiled. 'I can't very well imagine you making a mistake, sir.'

Tads hurried back. He had half hoped that Manners might have included Vassall in the school team, as no real importance attached to the game with the Old Boys, but when Manners had stated that he intended to play Morris at centre-forward he had raised no objection. Morris was a good, hard-working player and the best fellow in the position (except Vassall) available. As Vassall had played in the past, Morris was to be preferred, of course. There could be no argument.

But Tads was determined that this unlooked-for chance should be seized. The Old Boys arriving a player short was a veritable avalanche of luck. Nothing more opportune could possibly have happened.

He quickly found the boy for whom he was looking.

'Vassall, you may have a big chance to-day,' he started; 'how are you feeling?'

Vassall flushed.

'Quite fit, sir, thank you.' He looked questioningly. The words had sent a wild thrill of hope surging through him.

'I suppose you are wondering what I am getting at? Well, the Old Boys' team have arrived a man short—a centre-forward. If you would like to take it, I think I can get you the vacant place. You would be playing before Gilbert Laidlay, the old international,' he finished.

'Thanks awfully, sir.' Vassall's voice cracked.

'It will be a fairly stiff test.'

'I will do my best, sir—and try not to let you down—' His voice was full of determination.

'That's all right,' replied Tads, trying to keep voice steady and unaffected, whereas he was tremendously excited himself. 'You know Mr. Laidlay, you? I'll take you along to him.'

It was in this way that David Vassall came back into the sporting limelight, and remained for a couple of hours at least the central figure in as intriguing a football drama as the mind of a novelist had ever conceived.

I had hobbled out to the field to meet the Old Boys' team, and it was while I was waiting that Vassall up to me.

'I am going to play, Watney,' he said; 'Tads has got me another chance—I hope—and believe—I shall do better this time.'

'Play—for whom?' I had caught hold of his arm in my excitement. Play!—but the school team been chosen, and all the fellows were fit?'

'For the Old Boys—they came a man short.'

The significance of the thing struck me like a blow in the face. Here was a case of poetic justice being done with a vengeance. By skill and artistry Vassall was the only possible candidate for the school centre-forward berth. Because of his inherent weakness he had been passed over — justly, in a measure, I was bound to confess—but the gods had decided that another kind of justice should be done—and so the old Reps had arrived a man short, and Tads, the sportsman, had arranged that Vassall should "make up." What would the school say?

McPhail came strolling up. I told him the wonderful news—how wonderful it was to McPhail could be seen by his glowing eyes—and he immediately sped hot-foot away. The most energetic broadcaster in the shop was going to get to work.

I do not mind confessing that when I saw David Vassall stepping on to the field in company with the team of old Reps, some of whom at least had nationally-famous names, I felt my heart jumping. This was one of the most dramatic moments I had ever experienced. All around me fellows were chirruping, and eagerly discussing the situation. To them the position was intriguing: how much more dramatic was it then to me— who knew part at least of the secret which meant so much in Vassall's life? It only needs for me to say that Stanhope himself was playing centre-half for the school for you to visualize for yourself the situation in all its unique developments. And as Manners went up to toss with Laidlay he touched Vassall on the shoulder —a kindly action, typical of the school skipper. Some of the fellows started cheering when they saw it.

I want to make the attitude of Repington with regard to Vassall as clear as possible. The first fierce resentment against the fellow who had proved himself a funk-shy had died down. Vassall himself was liked; his quiet demeanour and the various stories (propaganda by McPhail) which had been circulated had informed Repington that personally he was a decent sort. It was only his behaviour on the footer field which called for criticism.

It was strange to see a boy lined up alongside of men, but we were able to forget that fact quite soon.

Laidlay had won the toss for the Old Boys, and Morris kicked off for the school. The inside-right back-heeled to Manners, at right-half, who was just behind, and the school skipper essayed to send out to his left wing.

But, before he could kick, an opponent was on him meeting him in a fair charge and whipping the ball from his toe. Before the dust had cleared we all saw it was Vassall.

Tads was standing beside me, and I heard him breathe a deep sigh of relief.

'Vassall! Vassall!'

The ranks of Tuscany were cheering him—this boy who was playing against, instead of for, the school! Speeding on, the Old Boys' centre-forward swept a long ball out to the right.

Here Longney, a famous winger, was waiting. He took the ball in his stride, raced round Russell, was at left-back for the school, steadied himself, then centred squarely.

Long Jenkins saw the danger and lumbered across at full tilt to defend his goal. Vassall must have seen him coming. Yet, although he was himself running at top-speed, he did not falter. The result was he got the ball on to the side of his head, which he twisted sideways.

'Oh!' cried the crowd.

Vassall had nearly scored in that opening minute, for the school goalkeeper had only kept that danger-laden ball from entering the net by jumping wildly to the right, and tipping the ball over the bar for a corner.

It interested—and thrilled—me to watch the crowd trying to adjust itself to this unexpected sensation. They had just witnessed a startling transformation— a known funk-shy changed into a forward whose dash and skill went hand in hand with unmistakable courage.

'He's done it!—it's wonderful!' I heard Tads mutter ecstatically to himself just as the corner which the school goalkeeper had conceded was being taken.

The flag-kick was cleared, but the excitement remained. Everyone had been taken by surprise at that splendid opening raid of Vassall's, and everyone—or almost everyone—was pleased.

With that typical crouching run familiar to football followers the country over, Gilbert Laidlay came dribbling through a ruck of opponents. He passed to Vassall, and the latter took the ball as he ran.

Manners came challenging, and another time Vassall would have pulled up. But now he went straight ahead, swerving so brilliantly that for the second time within a few minutes he left the School Captain standing. Again the cheers volleyed—weren't we watching a miracle?

I saw Vassall become tense; he was vibrant with enthusiasm. How could anyone gauge the effect that applause had upon him? Remember these were practically the first whole-hearted cheers that he had gained since he had been at the school—and that he had wrung them from the fellows who had been his severest critics.

Those volleying cheers must have gone to his head like wine. But while they stimulated, they did not appear to intoxicate. They furnished Vassall with an even greater zest than he had had before—but that was all.

Stanhope v. Vassall.

The game now seemed to resolve itself into a personal struggle between these two; to my eyes at least the duel between them was the game in epitome. In spite of the famous players that the Old Boys' side included, nothing else seemed to matter—not even the wonderful constructive play of Gilbert Laidlay, the visitors' centre-half.

It was a hard, relentless but perfectly clean duel—need I say that? It was as though Stanhope was resolved to test to the uttermost this surprising and new-found courage of the boy; whilst Vassall, on his part, seemed to appreciate the fact that he had a foe—a player who could appreciate at its true worth the skill he showed.

The crowd gasped and gaped. For they were seeing something which almost bowled them over with astonishment. As the play proceeded it became more and more evident that the whole course and result of the match hinged on how completely Vassall could outwit the man who opposed him.

Vassall had secured initial honours, but Stanhope was destined in after years to become one of the finest amateur centre-half-backs in the kingdom, and his greater experience enabled him to level matters up during the first twenty minutes.

Then the odds slumped in Vassall's favour again: he called upon other tactics and fresh wiles. These new tricks tested Stanhope to the limit; he found it increasingly difficult to hold the younger boy in leash. Vassall's footcraft was superb; the boy proved he could work the ball in an astonishingly small space.

Not that he became selfish; he was too good a footballer for that. And the instinct for the game which must have descended to him from his father told him when to part with the ball. He kept the two men playing on either side of him well supplied with passes as well as his wingers. In this respect he was a connecting link in a flexible chain.

But it was his penetrative power which caused most comment. He was always looking for a chance. A rather heavy buffeting which Jenkins, the school right-back, accidentally gave him half an hour after the start, did not dissipate the goal-seeking ardour of the metamorphosed Vassall.

I was afraid myself that this heavy fall—from which he got up white-faced and shaking—would take the steam out of him, bring back the old fears, the former nerves. I knew that Tads was afraid so, also—and you who read this can possibly imagine our delight when a minute after we saw Vassall make another spirited dash for goal.

This time—but that goal is worth description.

He had to beat both backs. But Russell was deceived by a pretence to pass, and then, increasing his speed, he endeavoured to sprint past Jenkins. The latter was no slouch, for all his awkward gait, when it came to a sprint, and the pair raced side by side, shoulder to shoulder, while the touch-lines were packed with madmen.

When about fifteen yards from goal, we saw Vassall nudge the ball in a bit and then raise his right foot.

'Goal!'

The cry seemed to split the sky. Hit truly, the ball had travelled like a brown bullet, wide of the school goalkeeper's right hand, and came to rest snugly in the lower right-hand corner of the net. A lovely, a beautiful goal! One to cherish in the memory and recall when one's spirits are low and one is inclined to think that all life is a mocking farce.

The Old Boys ran out winners by two goals to nil. Longney, the outside-right, scored the second with a swerving shot from the wing that he might have intended for a centre.

But the score—in itself—meant nothing. What did matter was that Vassal' had completely re-habilitated himself. How, no one knew—but that made the mystery all the more interesting , and the satisfaction to those of us who liked Vassal all the more enjoyable.

It was a wonderful triumph. I believe some of the Tads' fellows, headed by McPhail, would have carried Vassall off the field, if the centre-forward had not been immediately surrounded by members of the team he had led to victory.

I saw Gilbert Laidlay talking to Vassall. What it was I could not hear, but Vassall was blushing to his eyes, so that one was able to guess.

CHAPTER XXI

Tads has Another Talk

Changed, and feeling that he had never really lived until this minute, Vassall was going in to tea when he met Birtles face to face. Birtles scowled.

'Quite the little hero, aren't you?' he sneered; 'like the kid in the school yarn. But you needn't expect that *I'm* going to fall on your neck and join in the general rejoicing. Personally, I loathe you now just as much as I did before—perhaps a bit more—and what's happened to-day won't make any difference.'

'Thanks for telling me,' replied Vassall, to whom the words, after the afternoon's triumph, had come as a cold douche, 'but I haven't asked you to fall on my neck yet—and I am not likely to either. Anything more to say?'

'The rest can wait.' Birtles, with a frown, passed on.

The significance of this encounter had not been lost upon Tads, who had witnessed it. After tea, acting upon a resolve which had been forming in his mind for some time, he sent for Birtles.

The latter looked sullen as he came into the room.

'I thought I would have a little chat with you about football, Birtles—you've lost your keenness, haven't you? That seems rather a pity, for you used to be quite a useful back.'

Tads' tone invited confidence. There was nothing suspicious in it—but Birtles, all the same, was highly suspicious of this interview which he would have avoided if it had been possible. He had come to the house-master's room expecting a pi-jaw.

He did not want to answer a lot of embarrassing questions. Not that he was afraid—he would have faced the "sack" itself without a tremor—but he realized that in a cross-examination by Tads he would come out a very bad second-best. He would have to admit—and he was determined to admit nothing. He hated the swine Vassall; would always hated him more than ever because he owed the fact that he was still at Repington to him.

He decided to play safe, and to be as non-committal as possible. Perhaps then Tads would get sick of asking his blighted questions.

'I didn't play very well against Wyvern's,' he agreed; 'as a matter of fact, I was pretty awful. I knew that myself—before Stanhope rubbed it in.'

Tads drummed his fingers on the side of his chair.

'I saw the game,' he remarked; 'you did play badly—but you didn't look well, Birtles. You don't look well now—what's the trouble?'

'N-nothing, sir.' But into the face, which had become white, unhealthy, and almost flabby, crept a dull crimson stain.

'Birtles, I never believe in forcing myself upon a boy. And I never force a boy who doesn't want to do it to give me his confidence. But in your case I feel that it would be for your good if you gave me your confidence. Will you?'

The house-master had spoken earnestly. Birtles gulped. He appeared on the verge of making a quick and composed statement, but the words seemed to freeze on his lips.

'There's nothing to tell,' he mumbled; 'football isn't everything. I know I've been slacking—but I hate Stanhope just as I hate that precious pet of his, Vassall. And after being shouted at on the field—'

Tads changed his tactics.

'What is the trouble between you and Vassall, Birtles? You ought to get on all right together. You come from the same district, don't you?'

'Yes—worse luck.'

'Then what is the trouble?' persisted Tads.

'Why don't you ask Vassall—sir?'

'I thought I would ask *you*,' smiled the master.

'I hate him—that's honest, at any rate,' exclaimed Birtles.

'Very honest. But why? What has he done to you?'

'Nothing.' At the memory of what Vassall had done *for* him, he coloured again.

'So you won't tell me, Birtles?'

'There's nothing to tell.' He wasn't going to admit anything.

'Well, all right. But now I want to ask you if you think the game is worth the candle, Birtles?' Tads' voice had become cold and stern.

'What game?' But that tell-tale flush was still in his face.

'The game you have been playing for some time past—the dirty, rotten, beastly game that Small taught you. Thank goodness Small has gone now—he would have been thrown out of this school long ago only I could not get direct proof. It was Small who got you into trouble with that bookmaker, Joe Binks, wasn't it, Birtles?'

The boy was caught unawares, so swiftly had the question been asked.

'How did you know—has Vassall told you?' he exploded.

'Calm yourself. I have never discussed you with Vassall, and he has never discussed your affairs in my hearing. I got the information from quite another source.'

'I was just as much to blame—I wanted some money.'

Tads could not help admiring his refusal to go back upon his former associate, but he replied contemptuously: 'And like many another fool before you, you thought you could get it backing horses. Money isn't made that way, Birtles. How much do you owe now?'

'My father is going to pay it,' was the sullen answer.

'That's all right. If he hadn't been— if you had really been pressed, I mean—I would have offered to advance you the money myself. I should have been glad to do so—we can't have two expulsions from this house in one term, you know, Birtles.'

The boy started to reply, but appeal better of it. He remained silent.

'I don't want to preach—but think over whether your present attitude is worth all the clean, honest fun you are missing, Birtles. You were always fond of football—is it worth while giving up?'

But there was still no answer, and so Birtles left.

CHAPTER XXII

Birtles hears a Voice

Birtles remained for a long while in a brooding attitude after his interview with the house-master. Although Tads had not preached, he had shown conclusively that he considered he (Birtles) was in the wrong. The boy himself knew this to be so, but the realization did not bring composure of mind. He was in a highly dangerous state; he felt that he would like a thundering good row. After that he might be more at ease with himself and the world.

The opportunity for this explosion came sooner than he had anticipated. The next day, restless and nursing a slumbering hatred against everyone at Repington, he deliberately broke bounds. To do something contrary to law and order was necessary to his temperament that afternoon—and his face glowed with sullen satisfaction when he met Stanhope face to face.

Tads' Football Captain had been doing some hard thinking himself. The unsavoury episode of Small had sunk deep into his mind. To one who had a healthy pride in his house, the whole thing was an abomination and a disgrace. Much as he disliked Birtles in some ways, he did not wish the fellow to follow in the footsteps of the rotter Small. Yet that he seemed likely to do so was evident.

He stopped, and frowned.

'Of course, you know you are out of bounds, Birtles.

'Of course,' with a sneer.

'What's the idea?'

'That I jolly well intend to do exactly as I like in the future.'

'H'm.' Stanhope's frown became more pronounced. 'But, of course, you've got sense enough to know where that will lead you—in the same direction as your pal Small.'

Birtles flushed. Only he knew how foul a thing Small was, and it was horrible to have his personality linked with the other's in this way; but, acting up to the principle he had set himself, he determined not to give the Football Captain any more satisfaction than he had given Tads.

'What's that got to do with you? It's purely my affair, surely? I don't want any kindly shepherding or any rot of that sort, thank you,' sneering. 'I should think all your time in that direction was occupied in looking after your pet Vassall!'

'We can leave Vassall out of it. What I want to know is whether you intend to keep on being a silly ass? You're slacking all ways round.'

'It's my own affair.'

'Not while I'm skipper of footer,' sternly rejoined Stanhope. 'I have given you a pretty long rope, Birtles, because I hoped that you would come to your senses in time, but as you don't appear to be coming to reason I'm going to use other measures.'

'Report me to Tads for being out of bounds, suppose?'

'No—I shall try to lick you.'

At this unexpected answer Birtles smiled like one who has just received an extraordinary but totally unexpected and welcome piece of news.

'Now?' he inquired eagerly.

'Now,' replied Stanhope; 'but if I do lick you I shall expect you to turn out at footer again. Is that agreed?'

'Righto! Very pleased,' grinned Birtles, and took off his coat.

A few seconds later the "mill" was on. Stanhope was eager, but his opponent had a far better idea of boxing—he had received lessons at home from a professional—and very quickly he knew he had Stanhope's measure.

He experienced a grim and unholy satisfaction in smashing his football captain to the turf. Three times Stanhope rose only to be beaten to the ground again with a heavy blow scientifically aimed—and the last time he stayed down.

'Had enough?' inquired Birtles, assisting the other to rise.

'For the time being,' replied Stanhope; 'I always had an idea you were useful with your fists—well, we shall be able to use you in the house boxing; you ought to be quite a useful man.'

Without further comment Stanhope walked away. He reproached himself bitterly for being licked—not that he minded taking the whacking, but through being beaten he had lost any hold he might have had on Birtles. The latter would have kept to his promise of resuming training if he had been licked, but now he would go on playing the silly fool until in the end he would get the sack just as Small had done. It was a very disgruntled Stanhope who returned to Repington.

Birtles watched the boy he had beaten walk away and then flung himself down on the grass. It is one of the truisms of life that things never come up to the posters on the wall—there is a worm in every bud.

In this particular bud there was a rather large worm. Now that the heat of the conflict had died down, Birtles began seriously asking himself if he was glad or sorry that he had knocked the stuffing out of Stanhope? He assured himself that he was glad, but there was a small voice inside that told him he was a liar. 'Anyway, he jolly well asked for it,' he summed up in conclusion. But even that wasn't entirely assuring.

Birtles was by nature a breaker-up, an iconoclast. His mind was in revolt against settled law and order. The atmosphere at Repington fretted him. The truth was that he didn't share in the tradition of the place; things which were almost sacred, and certainly hallowed to boys whose fathers and grandfathers had been at Repington before them, chafed him. He wasn't at ease at the school; he felt himself an outsider because had never been admitted to the inner circles. So he affected to despise much that, given the chance, he would really have supported with all the strength he had.

He was not popular; he never had been popular. Perhaps if he had been popular, his nature might have changed. Outside of football, he was ignored even by members of his own house—apart from a few fawning sycophantic juniors who would have "sucked up" to any senior who showed the slightest inclination to talk to them.

It takes a crisis to move some minds—and the crisis had come to Birtles that afternoon. Strictly speaking, his fight with Stanhope had been only one in a series of crises, but it affected him most strongly. He knew that Stanhope would not report him for being out of bounds; it wasn't any fear about that which caused him to frown as he pulled at the cigarette which he had taken from the case in his pocket.

The fact was he was disappointed when he should have been triumphant. The victory he had gained was hollow. It now made him frown instead of smile. He didn't suppose that Stanhope had ever taken a boxing lesson in his life. He had; consequently he had started with an advantage. Not quite sporting, perhaps.

Stanhope must have wanted to lick him—must have longed to lick him very badly. Principally because, of course, he would have got him back into training for footer again. Now he would know there was no chance of that.

He had hit the fellow beastly hard too.

Altogether Birtles didn't enjoy his cigarette nearly as much as he had anticipated. It tasted bitter—almost sour.

It had taken some doing, but he was in the study.

'Look here, Stanhope, I'm not going to ask any favours, you understand, but if you want me I don't mind turning out for the house to-morrow.'

Stanhope, a thick strip of sticking-plaster above his left eye, looked up. There was nothing to be gained from his expression, however.

'Thanks for letting me know, Birtles—I'll think about it.'

'Oh—all right.' Somewhat taken aback, the volunteer turned abruptly on his heel, and left the room.

Once outside he called himself every kind of a fool for having offered his services. Although he had slacked, he was infinitely the best left-back in the house. Stanhope knew this as well as himself—and yet—

'He can do as he jolly well likes,' the volunteer muttered angrily as he turned away.

That was exactly what Stanhope did do, as the notice-board the next morning proved. Harptree was down to play at left-back against Canaver's that afternoon.

Birtles had the news brought to him. He had half-expected Stanhope to come to him, but the skipper had stayed away. In consequence of this, he had not allowed himself to be seen within recognizable distance of the notice-board.

Harptree!

Well, if Stanhope was fool enough to play a fellow who could only use one foot and who was weak in tackling, that was his concern. Only he needn't expect him to give any more concessions—the house football could go to the dogs for all he cared.

He made a point of not going near the playing-ground that afternoon. Once again he broke bounds.

Returning for tea he found the house ringing with the news that Tads had beaten the expected cock house 2-1; that Vassall had scored both goals, and that Harptree had done quite well in his old position of left-back.

'Splendid!' he sneered.

Inwardly he fumed, but he affected a complete indifference when Stanhope came into his study that night.

'I just want to tell you why I didn't play you this afternoon, Birtles,' started the skipper.

Birtles yawned, ostentatiously.

'My dear, good fathead, you needn't trouble; it doesn't interest me in the least. Why waste time and trouble, therefore, in calling on me?'

Stanhope ignored the gibe.

'You are a much better back than Harptree, of course,' he said, 'but you have been slacking for weeks now, and Harptree has been trying hard to get into the team. That was why I played him. If you go on training, Birtles—'

'Don't waste any sleep over that, Stanhope; I'm not going to train. Next term there will be boxing, and then I may. But not now—Harptree did very well this afternoon, so I'm told. Persevere with him, my friend; I will drop out.'

'Well, I've given you the explanation that I felt you were entitled to. It was a matter of principle.'

'Quite so! You're strong on principle. Wonderful thing when one doesn't overdo it.'

Birtles yawned again.

CHAPTER XXIII

Tads makes a Confession

With the Christmas holidays drawing near, Tads was faced with a problem. It was a difficult problem, but he had no intention of shirking it. As he saw it, a greater amount of good had resulted from the action—somewhat startling as this had been—which he had taken than if he had allowed matters to drift.

But it was essential, he decided, that he should see Mrs. Vassall, the mother of the boy in his house, and explain matters to her. The memory of what Gordon Watney had told him convinced him of this. Besides, he must clear the ground for Vassall himself; it would not be fair to let the boy face the music on his own. He must see Mrs. Vassall before her son arrived home.

'Here's a nice do,' cried McPhail, 'the guv'nor's hung up in some beastly outlandish spot in the Balkans—where are the Balkans, Vassall?— and won't be home for Christmas. He wants me to go to Aunt Millie's. Aunt Millie and I don't see eye to eye with each other on a good many things. *Ergo*: I shan't go to Aunt Millie's: I think I shall put up at a hotel in town.'

'I'm jolly well sure you won't!' replied Vassall, emphatically; 'if you can't spend Christmas with your father, you're coming home with me— that's settled!'

'Well,' grinned McPhail, 'I don't mind telling you that nothing would really suit me better—and —er—thanks very much!'

They both paid me a visit before their train left.

'See you next term, Watney, old horse!' said McPhail, with characteristic disregard for the grey hairs of his elders.

'Hope you both have a good time,' I said, wondering what would happen in that term to which McPhail was already looking forward, it seemed.

112

All through the journey, Vassall had seemed very preoccupied, and at last McPhail was forced to ask "what was eating him."

'American slang—very forceful,' Stanhope's fag supplied as a sort of marginal note.

Vassall pulled himself together. But it was rather shamefacedly that he replied: 'I say, McPhail, will you do me a favour?'

'Will I do what?—what is it you want, the earth, the Carlton Hotel, or any little trifle like that?'

'Oh, nothing so big as that—a different kind of favour, I mean. I don't want you to talk too much about football to my mother, if you don't mind. She—she doesn't like talking about football. You see—' Vassall did not finish. The fact that the train pulled up at that moment at a small country station may have stopped him.

McPhail did not pretend to notice the stoppage.

'Oh, certainly, old man,' he answered, but his tone was a trifle crestfallen. One of the many joys to which he had looked forward in going home with Vassall for the holidays was to talk to Mrs. Vassall about her son. And how on earth could one talk about David Vassall without bringing in his football? Absolutely imposs!—but still he had given his promise—had to give it—and, of course, he would keep it.

Sensing the mood (although not understanding it) that Vassall was in, McPhail confined his attentions for the rest of the journey to the bundle of amazingly assorted literature with which he had provided himself.

Vassall was thankful for this respite from his companion's incessant, although extremely amusing chatter. Now that he was nearing home—now that he would shortly be looking into his mother's face—he was seriously troubled.

He had broken his promise to his mother—the fact that circumstances had compelled him to do so was outside of the main question. He had promised his mother that he would not play football at Repington and—

Would his mother understand?—and would she forgive him? It might be difficult to get her to appreciate his point of view, when she had such a strong opinion of her own. There was the very best of reasons for this prejudice, of course—but—oh, it was going to be very difficult. She might be upset, although in every other way she was so splendid, and that would mean that not only would his holiday be spoilt, but that he would feel he could never forgive himself.

But, hang it, he couldn't keep on like this: he had his duty to his guest to perform. Already McPhail must be thinking that he was a pretty rotten sort of host.

'Here we are!' he exclaimed with more light-heartedness than he really felt, when the train drew up at his station at last; 'the mater is sure to be here,' poking his head out of the window, and glancing hurriedly up and down the platform.

But, to his great disappointment, only Tomkins, the chauffeur, showed up.

'No, Master David, Mrs. Vassall is quite well, thank you — but she said that she couldn't get away. Don't you worry; I'll see about the luggage, sir.'

'Some beastly visitor, I suppose,' Vassall confided to his guest, and the latter nodded sympathetically.

'Personally, I always hate my guv'nor to meet me on a crowded platform. He is so excessively affectionate. That sort of thing, it seems to me, should be done in the privacy of the home, not in full view of the populace, who always grin—in the intervals of their eating bananas.'

All the way home Vassall wondered what could have kept his mother from meeting him; in her last letter she had devoted a whole paragraph to the joy she would have in being on the platform to meet him on his return.

He had memorized the words in that paragraph as a lover recalls the words of his beloved. Vassall was very old-fashioned in the respect that he gloried in the love which the mother who idolized him had for her only son. Ever since he had been a small "kid" this love had existed between them. His mother had always called him "sweetheart"—just as though he had actually taken the place of her real sweetheart—his father—who was dead.

That love was safely locked inside him; never under any circumstances would he ever talk about it to anyone, for it was sacred to him—and no one could hope to understand; not even Watney, perhaps, who, in so many ways, had been a kind of elder brother to him.

He burst into the hall, closely followed by McPhail, directly the car stopped.

And then he had a tremendous shock.

For behind the outstretched arms of his mother was a man.

A man he knew—

Tads!

His mother smiled. Nothing was very much wrong then; that was all right, anyway. And the mystery—for it was a mystery—would be explained after he had had his tea. So, being hungry, and feeling that the world was still spinning on its axis in the old-fashioned way, he made a good meal—and the led McPhail out to make the acquaintance of Tinker, a Sealyham terrier, and undoubtedly the greatest dog in the world. Tinker, after a few preliminary sniffs, evidently approved of the Light of Repington, and, satisfied, Vassall went back into the house.

'Of course, you are surprised to find me here, Vassall,' started Tads, 'but, as I have already told your mother, I felt it was my duty to come and make a certain explanation to her. I have told her that it was due to me that you played football last term.'

He could not have that.

'It was my fault, Mother. I meant to tell you—I was going to tell you right away.'

Mrs. Vassall, turning to the house-master, smiled. The serene confidence of that smile—the faith in it; the joy, and the pride of possession! More plainly than words it said: 'You understand now why I am proud of my son; why I love him as I do. He would never try to deceive me.'

'I repeat it was my fault, Mrs. Vassall. David has nothing to be ashamed of—however strong your prejudice might have been against his playing. I have already told you how he fought against his fear on the field, and how, by some strange means, that fear was overcome. His position at the school—allowing for his temperament—would have been impossible if he had not played football. Although I recognize my grave responsibility in forcing your son to play football, Mrs. Vassall, at the same time I would point out to you that David here'—he smiled in the boy's direction—'has achieved a personal distinction at Repington which will be to the lasting credit not only of himself but of the school. I can assure you of this, Mrs. Vassall—that your son is a natural footballer, a boy born to play the game, and it was inevitable that directly he came to Repington, he *should* play the game.'

David looked at his mother. Tads was a brick once again; he had put forward a wonderful defence. But would it be strong enough to overcome his mother's years-old prejudice?

'I am very much indebted to you, Mr. Tadburn, for coming so far out of your way to tell me this,' Mrs. Vassall said. 'Since David has been at Repington I have been thinking how unfair it was of me to expect a strong, healthy boy like David to stop himself from playing football.

'I am afraid,' the speaker went on, 'that I have been, unconsciously it is true, dreadfully selfish about this matter. Indeed, at one time I did not think I could allow David to go to Repington. I realized something of the struggle he would have to put up when he got there. It was his uncle, my brother, who finally persuaded me. And I am glad now I consented—you are ever so much more of a man than when you left me, David! Will it content you, Mr. Tadburn, that I not only forgive you for what you have done for my boy, but—I thank you? If you knew the reason I had—'

'Mrs. Vassall, please do not distress yourself. And I think I already know the reason.'

'You do?'

'I think I do, Mrs. Vassall—but please do not discuss it, for I can realize how much sorrow it must give you. Now that I have your forgiveness for interfering with this young man's plans I'll be getting along.'

'Are you sure you won't stay? You would than welcome—wouldn't he, David?'

'Rather!' replied David with enthusiasm: 'I should like you to stop—awfully, sir.'

'That's jolly decent of you, but I can't, really. Oh, I should like to, no end—if you forgive the expression, Mrs. Vassall—but I am due in town to-night. Besides what with McPhail already here and Geekie coming later, you will be having your fill of visitors. If I may, I hope to drop in again after Christmas—I could manage that.'

In the hall Vassall, his hand in his house-master's became a trifle incoherent.

'Awfully good of you—I can't thank you enough—I don't know what I should have done with Mother—if—'

'Get back to her now: don't waste time on me!' replied Tads crisply.

CHAPTER XXIV

Quits

'This is where he went in; I feel sure it was,' said McPhail. Vassall looked thoughtfully at the small gap in the hedge.

'Well, if he doesn't come back soon I shall have to go after him, that's all,' he said. His tone was one of unshakable resolution. Tinker was not only his own pal, but his mother's inseparable companion. If anything should happen to him—but he wouldn't think about that.

'He's sure to come back.' McPhail, who was one of Tinker's staunchest supporters himself by this time, tried to be reassuring.

'He would in the ordinary way, but all this,' pointing over the hedge, 'is sporting land. There are all sorts of traps and gins, I daresay—'. Springing forward, he continued: 'What was that, Mac? I'm sure I heard Tinker howl!'

The two had gone for a walk this bright, crisp December morning and were now in the heart of the country. On the hill before them was a wood; from this wood game would rise every now and then with a whirring of wings. Standing sentinel on the other side of the hedge was a gaunt signpost, the stereotyped warning:

TRESPASSERS WILL BE PROSECUTED — By Order.

McPhail took one glance at this and cheerfully grinned.

'I haven't the pleasure of knowing Mr. Order he said, 'but if that was Tinker, we ought to be seeing about it; here's a bit where we can get through.'

But when he turned, he found that Vassall was already through the hedge.

'Tinker! Tinker!'

Racing forward, Vassall called for his dog; but it was not until they had run half a mile or so over the rough stubble that Tinker, a broad grin on his face came racing out from a covert. He looked as though he had been up to some mischief, and any magistrate would have convicted him on sight.

'Come here, sir!' cried Vassall sternly, and Tinker, his tail now between his legs and the grin changed to a look of appeal, took up a supplicatory position by his master's feet.

Vassall at once put the leash on him, and then, turning to McPhail, said: 'We had better be getting back, old man. I've just remembered whose land this is—'

He did not finish the sentence for, waving their arms excitedly, three men came rushing across at them. One was a short, very stout individual, dressed in a shooting suit, and the exertion involved must have been costing him dearly.

McPhail shaded his eyes with his hands.

'Do my eyes deceive me, Vassall, or do I see a faint resemblance to one Birtles, friend of our happy youth, in the rotund person trundling rapidly towards us?'

'It's Birtles's father,' explained his companion quickly. 'I was just going to tell you—I suddenly remembered that we were on his land. The thing is: what are we going to do? He hates me. Shall we cut and run for it? I don't think it likely that they could catch us up.'

McPhail immediately vetoed this proposition—which, it is but fair to say, Vassall had only half-heartedly put forward.

'Not on your life, old son,' replied Repington's leading light; 'I have never seen a brewer in the flesh before, and however unpleasant the sight may be, I am resolved to undergo the sensation. And who knows? Friend Birtles himself may be lurking in the background. Nothing would give me more pleasure than to exchange a hearty Christmas greeting with that scion of the Hops Trust!'

'Shut up, you ass!' exclaimed Vassall, doubled up with laughter.

'Ah! But you'll laugh on the other side of your face in a minit or two!' roared an angry voice; 'wot do you mean by deliberately trespassing on land that you've bin warned off, eh?'

'If you will take your hand off my shoulder I will try to give you an explanation,' Vassall said quietly to the gamekeeper, who was already beginning to manhandle him.

'What does the impudent young rascal say, Timms?'

The rotund gentleman, whose exertion had caused great beads of perspiration to appear on his highly-coloured face and forehead, came forward.

'My friend remarked that he could explain why we were here, sir,' McPhail said quietly.

James Birtles swung round.

'What was that? Don't you be impertinent, you young jackanapes!'

'I am not being impertinent, sir,' replied McPhail quietly. 'I shouldn't advise you to put your hand on me,' he warned the second gamekeeper, who had advanced a step or two in his direction at assign from the brewer.

Vassall now addressed himself to the latter.

'Our trespassing was quite an accident, sir.' he explained. 'We were out for a walk with Tinker, my Sealyham here, when he got away through a gap in the hedge. I heard him howl—or fancied so—and, being afraid that he might be caught in a trap or a gin, I—we, rather—followed him. Directly he came to heel I put the lead on him, as you can see.'

'I don't believe a word of it! You were after my game! I'll have the law on you—Ah! what's that?' For another gamekeeper had drawn near carrying a dead bird in his hand.

'Killed by that blighted dog, sir—you can see that for yourself!' the man added maliciously.

'You see!' roared the brewer, waving the bird like a maniac. 'I'll have the law on you, I say! You came here after my birds, and then tell me a pack of lies!— Get out, you murdering brute!' he raised his foot to kick Tinker, who was snarling softly at him.

Vassall tugged the dog backward.

The brewer's eyes gleamed.

'What's your name?' he rasped, pointing finger at Vassall.

'Vassall,' replied the latter. He was not going to lie.

'That settles it,' he said. 'Timms, go and ring up the police—I'll have these young blackguards locked up before I'm an hour older. It's a clear case of trespass and theft I have against them.'

'Theft?' retorted Vassall indignantly.

'Theft, I said. You send your cussed dog in here to kill a bird, and then if I hadn't come on the scene you would have made off with the bird —it's as clear as daylight.'

'On the contrary, it's absolutely and hopelessly muddy, sir, if you will allow me to say so,' commented McPhail; 'but never mind that. Call for the police, if you want to. We shan't attempt to get away, shall we, Vassall?'

'No,' said his companion. Vassall realized that the brewer knew he hadn't a fair case against them, and he didn't want it thought that he was afraid of a man who was petty enough to wreak vengeance upon a boy for a misunderstanding he had had with that boy's mother.

'What shall I do please, sir?' Timms, the gamekeeper, evidently knowing his master's erratic moods, had not yet departed on his quest for the police.

'Do? What I tell you!' exploded the brewer. 'Eh? What's that?' he demanded, for his sleeve had been suddenly pulled.

'Do what, guv'nor? What's going on here?'

McPhail was the first to recognize the newcomer who had put the question.

'Why, bless me old eyes, if it isn't Master Birtles!' he cried with an extravagant gesture of surprise; 'Master Birtles home from school! And how the lad's grown, to be sure! Well, well, well!'

Contenting himself with a malignant glare in McPhail's direction, Birtles turned again to his father.

'What's happened here?' he asked again.

'You may well ask that, my boy,' exploded his father. 'I find these two young blackguards trespassing on my land first of all. Then Jones finds a dead bird—killed by that blasted dog of theirs. And you see who one of them is, don't you?'

'Yes,' answered his son, looking at Vassall; 'I see who it is.'

To Vassall there was the suggestion of a veiled threat in the words, and he was quick to answer it.

'You certainly ought to know me by this time, Birtles,' he remarked.

'Would you be so kind, Birtles,' now remarked McPhail, 'as to suggest that if your father intends to send this worthy soul, Timms, for the police, he should do so at once? I'm tired of standing talking here.'

'You didn't mean that, guv'nor?' asked Birtles of his father.

'I certainly meant it! Timms—'

'Don't be foolish, Father. You can't do a thing like that. You surely had an excuse for coming here?' He looked at Vassall, who stared back. This was a new Birtles, and one he had not known before.

'Certainly I have an excuse. I have already given it to your father. McPhail and I, out for a walk with my dog, missed Tinker. He had crept through a gap in the hedge on to this land. I knew it was laid down to game, and I thought there might be traps and things in which the dog could get caught. Hearing him—or fancying I heard him—howl, I was afraid he was caught in something and so I cut across. As for the dead bird, I don't know anything about that—but I'm willing to compensate your father for the loss of it if necessary. I should have apologized if only he had been willing to admit in the beginning that I was speaking the truth. However, now he can do what he likes—only I would suggest, with McPhail, that he makes up his mind—I don't want to be too late for lunch.'

Birtles swung round on his father.

'You can't send for the police,' he said; 'it would be a rotten thing to do.'

When, grumbling, the brewer forced himself to be persuaded, Birtles came across to Vassall.

'I know the guv'nor had no real case against you, but all the same it might have been awkward if he had sent for the police—as, no doubt, he intended to do. Being only a self-made man, he could have stood the notoriety—I don't suppose it would have affected him the least little bit—but I don't expect your mother would have liked to have had her son arrested.

'We're quits now, Vassall,' went on Birtles; 'quits over that motor-cycle job. Don't express any thanks because I don't want them. And understand this: that I only did what I have done because I hate the thought of being under any obligation to you—a fellow I still detest and loathe! This won't make any difference—there's no more chance of our being friends in the future than there was in the past!'

Having said this, the astonishing Birtles walked away.

'Come on, Mac,' said Vassall. If Birtles had remained, he would not have known what to have said to him.

'I must say,' commented McPhail, 'that Birtles came out rather decently in this stunt, even though he could not let the chance slip to tell us about it. He's thorough, anyway—I don't suppose he'll go back on what he said just now. We shall hear from him again next term, I'm thinking.'

'No doubt,' replied Vassall. 'The father showed himself such a poisonous brute to-day, because, I believe, my mother did not return the call which Mrs. Birtles—who is even a worse horror than the brewer—paid when she first came into the district. They weren't the mater's sort, and although she isn't a snob she didn't want to get mixed up with them. The Birtles evidently resented it, and that is the reason, I suppose why Birtles has always tried to be as rotten as possible to me at Repington. But it's all wiped out now, I hope.'

'Wait until next term before you say that,' commented McPhail sapiently.

CHAPTER XXV

Soul Searchings

It was jolly coming back after the holidays—jolly meeting old friends, seeing old faces, exchanging reminiscences with Stanhope, Manners, and the others. I suppose it was due to my game leg, and the fact that, as the onlooker, I saw behind all the scenes, that I had such vivid impressions about the shop. My father, an old Rep himself, smiled at my burning enthusiasm for the school, and the joy life in it gave me.

'You ought to be writing a book about Repington,' he had said during the holidays, and when I replied (somewhat shamefacedly, I am afraid) that I might do so in the future, he told me that he would place a copy on the handiest shelf of his book-case if ever the volume saw the light.

The first night of the return saw me as usual in Stanhope's study: I always went there like a ship coming into harbour.

'Hullo, Dot-and-carry!' called out Stanhope, 'bless your old face! What sort of a time did you have in the hols?'

'Ripping, thanks—and you?'

'Oh, so-so. Glad to be back, you know.' His face momentarily clouded, and I mentally kicked myself for being such an ass as to ask the question. But I had forgotten that the football skipper had once confided to me that his home life was none too pleasant. His father had married again not long after Stanhope's mother had died—married an actress, and —but there's no need to go into it. A rotten story of incompatibility of temperaments and all the rest of it.

'Hullo, Watney! Back in the old home again, then?'

McPhail, grinning, had come to report himself, and, as was his custom, to take part in any sporting consultations that might be under discussion. It was good to see the red-headed imp once more.

'I hear you've been up to some more mischief during the holidays,' Stanhope said, turning to his fag.

'Yes,' agreed McPhail, 'Birtles's father is even funnier than B. himself. Perhaps I ought not to tell that story, though—yes, I will,' he added hastily 'because it will show you that friend Birtles isn't quite as bad as what some of you might imagine.'

'H'm,' said Stanhope, very thoughtful.

'It was like this,' went on the fag, evidently anxious to tell his tale. 'Vassall and I went for a stroll one morning with Tinker, Vassall's Sealyham terrier—a nailing good ratter. Tinker gets away, and then we hear a howl. Vassall, who would give his right arm for the canine—which happens to be a close pal of Mrs. Vassall's, incidentally—begins to get fretful, and says that the land on which Tinker has strayed is full of traps, gins, and other contraptions not healthy for Sealyhams—it was laid down to game, you see.

'Vassall doesn't waste much time thinking; he up and he does! Hopping through the hedge, we try to find the faithful Tinker—get the situation?

'Directly we find the dawg, we are ourselves found—by a portly, red-faced cove, who turns out to be the brewer-father of our own dear Birtles! He is accompanied by two gamekeepers, and is exceedingly nasty—oh, very nasty! The things he said he was going to do to us!' McPhail chuckled at the reminiscence.

'Well, get on with it,' exhorted Stanhope, 'what about Birtles?'

'I am coming to him,' replied the tale-spinner; 'at the present time he has not made his appearance upon the stage. Well, here was the position: Birtles Paterfamilias was just sending one of his gamekeepers for the police—he had charged us with unlawful trespass, and the dog with killing a bird, I should explain—when up strolls B., junior—our own B., in short.

'I must say,' said McPhail, 'he was very decent—although, of course, we really hadn't done anything to cause a shindy. But you know how he showed he hated Vassall all last term, and one would have thought that he would have been only too anxious to get his dig in. He didn't do anything of the kind, as a matter of fact, for when the foaming brewer—I say that's not too bad, is it?—well, as I was remarking, when B. senior trots out this threat of sending for the police, B. junior tells him quite frankly that he is a fool and ought to know better. He saved the situation—because Vassall had determined not to cut and run: he meant to face it out. Well, there's the yarn, gents. What is your verdict?'

'Of course it was the only thing Birtles could have done,' commented Stanhope at once; 'if he hadn't stopped his father from making a fool of himself he ought to have been kicked out of the shop like his precious pal, Small!'

I was surprised at the bitterness of the skipper's tone; but at this time I did not know the whole story of his conflict with Birtles.

'But consider the circumstances, Skipper,' said McPhail, before I could make any remark myself; 'everyone knows that Birtles is a bit of an outsider socially. His father may brew the best beer in Christendom, but he's an impossible bounder—made his money in the War, and all that sort of thing—and the son takes after him. I strongly disapprove of Birtles myself, but I must say that I think he was rather decent on this occasion. Funny thing he said to Vassall after, though.'

'Go on—if it isn't confidential.' Stanhope was very plainly interested.

'Oh, I don't know that it's confidential—it affects the house. What he said was this, breathing low like the villain in the "drammer": "Now we're quits Vassall! But you don't expect me to fall round your neck and be friends because I hate you still—and I always shall hate you!" and that after Vassall once saved him—' The speaker stopped.

'Well?' persisted Stanhope.

'Skipper, I ought not to have said that. Vassall wouldn't like it if I told that bit. But you can take it from me all the same that Birtles ought to go down on his hands and knees to Vassall occasionally. Not that he ever will, of course.'

Stanhope pretended to be busy.

'Thanks very much for your yarn, McPhail; it was quite interesting. But you'll be wanting to cut back to your own quarters now; Watney and I are going to have a pow-wow.'

When the door had shut behind the fag, Stanhope leaned across and put his hand on my shoulder.

'As I said just now, Watney, it's good to see you old face again. When the time comes for us to chuck all this,' he looked round the well-remembered room affectionately, 'I hope that we shall still see a good deal of each other.'

'I hope so too, Skipper,' I said. Stanhope had always been one of my best friends; I admired him apart from the playing-field, and the thought of Tads' without him was not pleasant.

'I expect I shall be gone before you,' I said; 'next term will probably be my last.'

Stanhope bit his lip.

'*This* will probably be my last term, Dot-and-Carry!' he replied bitterly.

I started.

'But surely—' I began when he interrupted.

'I know. I thought I should last out for another football season. But —well, you're the only fellow in the shop I could possibly tell—but there was some unpleasantness at home about me this Christmas. The guv'nor's a brick. If he had his way he would let me go on to Oxford, but my stepmother objects, is apt to become personal, begrudges the money necessary to keep me here—and says that I am old enough to be earning my own living. So I'm chucking it at the end of this term; it is the only thing I can do in the circumstances, don't you see?'

I saw only too clearly.

'What a beastly business,' I muttered.

'It is in a way. I was going in for the Diplomatic Service—and now I suppose I shall have to become a pro. footballer instead. Not that I would mind that; I should love the life.'

There seemed nothing that I could say, and so I kept silent while Stanhope did some ruminating

'I'm telling you this for two reasons, Watney. The first is that I felt I had to talk to you about it—although I want you to keep it strictly to yourself—and secondly I want you to understand how keen I am, this being my last term, that Tads' should become cock house at soccer. My hat! if I could think that Tads' could win that Corinthians' Cup, I wouldn't mind going; I should have helped to do something, at all events.'

'You have done a tremendous lot, Stanhope, while you have been here.' I said what I and what I believed, but the skipper only shook his head.

'Not half as much as I should have liked—but then I suppose that is always the case. Anyhow, now that you know what is in my mind, what do you think about the prospects of our pinching that cup?'

'Vassall, if he doesn't go back, ought to be the most dangerous forward in the shop,' I replied.

'Yes—if he doesn't go back. Rather a marvellous business that, you know—a funk-shy changing in the way Vassall did towards the end of last term. Any ideas about it?'

'I think Tads had a great deal to do with it.' Beyond that I wouldn't say because I simply didn't know. The change was a complete mystery to me.

'I'm banking on Vassall in the forwards and Jenkins—'

'By the way, I haven't seen Jenks yet, Skipper.'

'He can't have turned up yet, otherwise he would have been here. He lives a goodish step away, don't forget. He may be here to-morrow, trust old Jenks for not turning up.'

The door opened and Tads appeared—to be greeted with acclamation by us both.

After the tumult had died down, the house-master, I noticed, was looking unusually serious.

'I am afraid I have some rather bad news for you, Stanhope,' he said.

'Bad news, sir?' Just as he was looking forward!

'Yes, Jenkins won't be back this term—not for some time. He's broken his leg.'

'*Broken his leg!*' The skipper's tone was heart-rending.

'Fell out of a tree, or something of that sort. Dreadful nuisance—but we shall have to make the best of it. It's a good thing Harptree is pretty useful.'

But when Tads had gone, Stanhope turned to me, and gasped:

'He doesn't understand! Harptree is not a patch on Jenkins, and in any case he is a *left*-back, not a *right*! And even then that's only *one* back when we want *two*—and two jolly good 'uns, too!'

'Birtles?' I suggested.

Stanhope almost groaned.

'There's the rub,' he said passionately; 'will he play? You remember last term?'

'Yes, I remember; of course you could *make* him play. Pressure could be brought to bear. You're skipper of the house football.'

'Neither Tads nor I would care for that method. That kind of thing is all right to read about in a certain kind of so-called school story, but it won't work in actual life. What sort of a game do you think Birtles would put up if he were forced to play? And, if he slacks this term as he did last, he won't be fit to kick a ball. No, the thing must be left to his conscience —if the fellow's got one.'

'I can't help thinking that he has—even if it may be a bit out of condition,' I said.

'Well, we shall see. Personally, I have my doubts. My own belief is that when he realizes the true state of affairs—how necessary it is that he should turn out—he will scoff, and go off smoking those rotten fags of his out of bounds. I'm not saying this because he gave me a licking last term—'

'Gave you a licking!' This was the first official intimation, although I had had my suspicions.

'A peach,' smiled Stanhope grimly; 'yes there's no doubt the fellow can box. He was out of condition but he fairly wiped the floor with me. He did come to me in a lordly fashion afterwards and offer to turn out against Canaver's, but because he wasn't fit to play in my opinion owing to his slacking, and because it wasn't good for discipline, in any case—I picked Harptree instead. I explained this as patiently as I could to Birtles, but he went off and sulked. And my opinion is that he will sulk this term as well as last.'

I stared at the wall. Curious how things had turned out—curious, but disappointing. Birtles, if he had had the planning of events, could not have made himself more master of the situation than he threatened to be now. I began to see him as a shadowy but cynical sort of minor Napoleon holding the destiny of Tads' in his hand. A fanciful picture, perhaps, but justified in a measure.

'Why not see him, Skipper?' I asked.

Stanhope frowned.

'Yes, I'll see him—I'll put myself in his way, anyhow. But, if the man has any sense of sportsmanship, any regard for the house, he will come to me himself.'

CHAPTER XXVI

Referred to Tads

According to this reasoning, Birtles's sense of sportsmanship was undeveloped, for he made no offer to Stanhope; and when the football skipper passed his way he affected not to see him.

The trouble lay in the fact that each was waiting for the other to make the first advance. Birtles knew where his duty rested, but he argued that he had once made an offer and it had been refused. It was up to Stanhope now.

Although he determined to train for the shop Boxing Championships which were due to come off that term, Birtles did not immediately set about the business of getting himself fit. Therein he made a mistake. A bad mistake. To have stopped him from brooding, he should have gone into training at the gym. As it was he smoked far too many cigarettes, broke bounds continuously—and felt altogether fed up with life in general and with himself in particular.

There was one thing Birtles would have liked to do; one thing he would have given anything to do—that was to play football again. But his pride and obstinacy, in the absence of Stanhope making any advance, proved the obstacle.

After the first week he became violently bored by his course of action. He simply ached to get his boot to a ball.

Drama, so the quidnuncs say, is the result of the clash of character upon circumstance. It may be so, but certainly something vital in the history of Tad: happened the second week of the term.

Somehow or other the story had leaked out that Birtles wouldn't play football, not because he had been dropped—everyone knew that. Stanhope could not really afford to drop him—but because he was a "rotten cad" as Featherstone, in characteristic phraseology, put it.

This statement, of course, spread like wildfire. McPhail had given it out that Stanhope had set his heart upon the house winning the

Corinthians' Cup that term, and, although the possibility seemed remote, even a wretched junior like Greenslade (with whom it will be remembered McPhail had a brief but spirited passage-at-arms earlier in this history) felt that it was up to everyone in the house to do all that was humanly possible with the object of achieving this laudable ambition.

A remarkable reversal of public opinion occurred: Birtles, owing to his very noticeable slacking, took the place formerly held by Vassall as the most disliked person in the house! Vassall, owing to his triumph over his inherent weakness, and the brilliant form he had shown in the match in the Old Boys' team, was now popular with the masses—and would have been more popular if he had gone out for the suffrages of the juniors.

The knowledge, on both counts, was gall and wormwood to Birtles. To be greeted by the devastating words of "Slacker!" and "Rotter!" from every hidden corner fretted his overwrought nerves until he could hardly keep himself in check.

A crisis was inevitable, and it came one afternoon in the hour preceding tea.

It had rained all that day, and no one could go out without risking a thorough drenching. The boisterousness of the juniors, imprisoned by the weather, had to be worked off somehow.

Wet weather always made Birtles feel particularly diabolical, and when the long-drawn-out and hateful word s-l-a-c-k-e-r! was heard in a penetrating howl outside his study door, he made one wild dive in search of a victim.

Scrambling to his feet was Peter McPhail. In the distance could be heard the wild scamper of retreating footsteps.

Birtles did not stop to consider if it was the boy he saw who had cried the taunt. *Someone* had howled that word—and McPhail was on the spot. That fact was sufficient evidence to Birtles who, catching the boy by the collar, pulled him into his study.

Flinging McPhail against the table, Birtles scowled at him.

'So it was *you!* Well, I've had enough of it, and I'm going to teach you that it's dangerous playing the fool with me.'

McPhail did not seem so impressed as the other would have wished.

'May I suggest,' he said coldly, 'that if you are in a bashing mood, Birtles, you should get someone more about your own weight and size.'

'Vassall, for instance?' sneered Birtles.

'Yes—I think Vassall would do very nicely. Of course, you are heavier—a good deal heavier now that you've been slacking for so long—'

The mention of that infuriating word drove Birtles almost to the point of madness. Savagely catching hold of the other's arm, he twisted it until McPhail had to cry out. Then, while the tears of pain were still standing in the fag's eyes, he hurled him viciously across the room.

'I'll half-kill you if you say I am a slacker again! he threatened.

'Well—aren't you?'

'No one in this house is going to call me a slacker,' persisted Birtles, rather taken aback at the other's unflinching attitude.

'But you can't deny that you are a slacker, Birtles. Hang it, no one but a slacker would moon about as you are doing when the team wants you to play football.'

'You had better stop it!' the other warned him darkly.

'Stop it!' replied McPhail, warming to his subject, 'that is exactly what you ought to do! You wouldn't be a bad chap if you only gave yourself a chance, Birtles—you proved that all right at Merrywood. But now you are a slacker, and you know it!'

Scuffling outside the door served to make Birtles determine on his course of action. If the kids listening outside had heard the words, and he allowed them to pass, he would never get any future peace.

Birtles moved resolutely forward.

'You've had this coming to you for a long time, McPhail, only perhaps you haven't realized it. Once Stanhope interrupted it—but there will be no of that now. Get across that chair—I'm going to teach you not to be so free with that cursed tongue of yours.'

The speaker picked up a walking-stick that was resting in a corner of the room, and pointed to a chair.

McPhail declined the invitation.

'Not likely,' he replied, shrugging his shoulders. Be lammed by a swine like Birtles? Not much!'

'I should advise you to,' said Birtles, more darkly.

'Thanks, Birtles, but I have always found my own advice best to follow. And my own advice in the present case is distinctly against bending over that chair,' McPhail spoke slowly, but distinctly. The usual "cheek" in his voice was absent, but he was determined enough.

Birtles did not wait any longer, rushing straight at his victim. He caught McPhail by the throat and swung him round. Then he started to belabour his victim with the stick.

In the turmoil some of the blows fell on the elbows which McPhail had thrust out in the endeavour to free himself. They were painful blows in the extreme, and the fag yelled.

'Come on!' shouted a voice outside.

The next moment the study was full of figures. These flung themselves on Birtles with a wild rush (they had to be quick, or their courage would have failed them) and a noisy conflict ensued.

The row reached the ears of Stanhope sitting in his study. Annoyed that his peace should be disturbed in this way, he hurriedly left his room, and walked down the corridor.

'*Birtles!*'

His voice rang with a startled rage. The former left-back of the football team was hitting out to right and left regardless of where the blows landed

The sound of the Football Captain's voice restored order and quietness.

Then a voice piped:

'Please, Stanhope, he was bullying McPhail, and so we rushed in. McPhail was yelling; we thought he was being killed.'

'Clear out!' rejoined Stanhope, and because his voice was kind, and because these juniors knew the skipper and liked him, they instantly obeyed.

'Not you, McPhail,' and the fag remained.

The sight of the damage McPhail had sustained infuriated Stanhope against the boy who now glared at him.

'Clear out yourself, you confounded ass!' cried Birtles. 'Do you want another licking, because I shall be only too pleased to give you one? What right have you to butt in here? Get out of my study before I throw you out!'

'I'm here as Captain of the House—if you like to question my authority you can go to Tads—he will enlighten you on the point, no doubt. And as Captain of the House I'm going to stay here until I received an explanation of this charge of bullying, Birtles. This is the second time you have bullied McPhail. I won't waste breath by telling you you ought to be ashamed of yourself for being such a cad—but I would remind you that the Head is rather down on bullies.'

'He cheeked me—shouted "slacker" outside my door.'

'Is that right, McPhail?'

'No,' replied the fag at once; 'what happened was this: I was coming down the corridor on the way to your study when a crowd of juniors, racing the other way, knocked me down. Someone outside Birtles' door shouted "slacker!" but it wasn't me. The door opened and Birtles rushed out and collared me. He lugged me inside and commenced lamming me. Then I asked him if he wasn't a slacker? He didn't reply, but told me to get across a chair. I wasn't going to stand any more of it, and so I refused.

131

Then he banged me with that stick—and then the crowd rushed in. I didn't call them—but I may have yelled; I'm not denying that.'

'So what it amounts to is this, Birtles,' commented Stanhope sternly. 'Just because you were in a beastly temper, you seized on the first junior you could catch, and commenced bashing him, without troubling to find out whether he was the proper person.'

'He cheeked me; that's enough,' was the sullen response, 'and I have already told you to clear out of my study.'

'All right—if that is your attitude! I now ask you as Captain of the House, to come along to *my* study. You can clear, McPhail.'

Left alone, the two seniors stared hard at each other.

'Suppose I don't,' said Birtles.

'If you don't, I shall go straight to Tads,' was the uncompromising answer; 'I didn't before—but I shall this time. You know what that will mean. He will probably go to the Head.'

Before the blurred mind of the other came a painfully vivid picture—of his father standing on the hearthrug in his library at Merrywood, cut to the heart because of the disgrace his son had brought upon his name. For himself he did not care—he never had cared—but he could visualize his father's distress when he knew that his only son had been expelled from the "gentleman's school."

'I'll come,' he said, gulping.

Inside his study, Stanhope picked up a cane.

'I'm going to give you a chance, Birtles,' he said, speaking not as Stanhope, but as Captain of the House; 'get over that chair, and take a dozen, and I won't anything to Tads.'

Blood leapt into the other's face.

'You propose to lam me?' he cried.

'Yes.'

'I'll see you to blazes first!—I'll kill you first!'

'Then I'm going to Tads. That is the only alternative left, Birtles.'

'This is a very serious matter, Birtles,' said Tads. 'You realize probably what would happen if I went the Head?'

'Yes, sir.'

'What made you forget yourself?'

The fury which had been raging ever since the commencement of the storm now burst forth. Birtles had come to the end of his self-control. The scene in Stanhope's study had taken a heavy toll of his nerves. He looked at the house-master and felt that he could talk to him.

'I don't know, sir. I must have been mad at the time. I'm not trying to make any excuses. I don't want you to think that. But I've been fed up ever since I came back. I wanted to play football, but I wasn't going to let Stanhope know. At the end of last term I told him I would play against Canaver's—and then he left me out. That finished me—I wasn't going to try to get any favours; if he didn't want me he could jolly well do the other thing.

'Then they began to call me a slacker. I was, I suppose—but I wasn't going to have the juniors calling after me. This afternoon when I heard someone shouting outside my study I rushed out and saw McPhail. Naturally enough, I thought it was he who had shouted. I knew that he hated me because of Vassall. Then—but I've told you I must have been mad, sir.'

'Well—sit down, Birtles.'

Only a man who understood the complexities of boys' natures would have been able to comprehend, but Tads saw the tortured workings of this boy's mind quite clearly.

'This must never in any circumstances occur again, you understand, Birtles?'

When Birtles had nodded in acknowledgment of that fact the house-master went on: 'Stanhope has not said much to me, but you have been in the wrong all the way through. What started you slacking, in the first place?'

Birtles muttered something to the effect that he did not know.

'The fault was yours to begin with—but I have no wish to rub it in. Would you like to get back into the team now?'

'I wouldn't ask Stanhope—no favours—' The rest was inaudible.

'There will be no need for you to ask Stanhope. If you will get yourself in shape again, I will speak to Stanhope myself. What do you say?'

What Birtles said was confused, but he appeared to be glad and grateful, and that satisfied Tads.

CHAPTER XXVII

The Return

The return of Birtles to Tads' team marked an occasion, for it was the second match with Lorimer's and the sporting feud between these two houses had always been marked.

The juniors had left the back alone after the afternoon of the scuffle. The news had leaked out that Birtles was resolved to do the decent thing, that he was going into strict training—had actually been seen in the gym. That could mean only one thing: he had finished with his rotten slacking. In these circumstances the past was wisely forgotten. Besides, with Birtles back in the team, Tads' chances were appreciably higher. Let the past bury its dead was the unspoken decision of the house.

'Watney, you are going to see the match afternoon, I suppose?'

I smiled at the question.

'Yes, sir—I think I shall be there.'

This brief talk had taken place in the morning. It had become something of a joke with Tads to ask me if I intended to watch the house football matches; he knew very well that even if I had to be carried to touch-line I should get there.

As we stood side by side watching the house captains toss, the memory came back of the first match we had played with Lorimer's. Then Vassall had funked so badly and so obviously that my heart had ached for the chap.

It was a different Vassall which we now saw trap the ball with the easy grace of a craftsman, during the preliminary kick-in, before crashing a rasper against the cross-bar.

Tads must have read what was in my mind, for he suddenly remarked: 'I wonder if he will follow his father and play for England — I should not be surprised. But it will be the first time that it has ever been done.'

A burst of wild cheering announced that Stanhope had won the toss. There was a little wind, and he elected to kick with it.

As the team took up its position, I noticed that Stanhope paused to exchange a few words with Birtles. The latter nodded.

'I am glad that matter has been fixed up,' said Tads.

This was a very different Birtles to the one we had seen lately. Report said that he had trained hard, and I was quite ready to believe it. The scowl, that had threatened to become habitual with him, had left his face, which was now normal and marked only by a stern determination. He had listened attentively, I recalled, to what the skipper had said to him. Decidedly this was a new Birtles.

While the referee took a last glance at his watch before blowing his whistle for the fray to commence, I had a long look down the touch-line. Everywhere were strained, tense, eager faces. Tads' to a man had caught the whole-hearted enthusiasm of their captain. To do or die: that seemed the spirit. Tads' had been cock house at footer before, and it was determined to be so again.

Prrrh!

Now the game was on—on to a running accompaniment of eager comment and frequent bursts of applause.

Early it was seen that Lorimer's were taking no chances with Vassall. The fellow might have been a funk-shy, but they had seen too much of him playing against the school for the Old Boys to give him any rope; Padmore, the hefty centre-half of the opposition stuck to him closer than a brother, shadowing him wherever he went.

'I wonder—?' started Tads to me.

But he needn't have wondered: Vassall had climbed the heights and was not going to slip down into depths again. He never funked Padmore —not even when the centre-half sent him reeling with a shoulder-charge into which he must have packed every ounce he carried.

Nerves were going to play an important part in this game; that was soon seen. There was too much on for some of the players to do themselves justice. While Vassall did not appear to be unduly affected, playing a cool clever game whenever he could slip Padmore, some of our fellows allowed the excitement to get them distinctly edgy. Our forwards could not seem to get going: Geekie messed several splendid sweep out to him from his centre. One ball he allowed to go clean through his long legs, and while Lorimer's crowd yelled with delight, Tads' supporters groaned.

After the first quarter of an hour, during which Lorimer's had done far too much pressing for my liking, Tads summed up the situation as follows: 'This is going to be a tremendously tough fight, Watney. Everything will depend upon two fellows, it seems to me—Birtles and Vassall.'

I followed his meaning. Would Birtles be able to keep the opposition out, and would Vassall be able to get through? That was the situation in a nutshell.

This game was destined to be Birtles's testing. Harptree, his partner, was not displaying the form that he showed when he played against Canaver's at the end of the previous term. He was painfully hesitant, and was often caught in two minds. The fact that he had the best Lorimer's forward against him was not helpful.

It was Gunn, this outside-left, who opened the score. Receiving from his left-half, he tricked Harptree with an ease that made us groan, and then centred. Birtles's head averted the danger temporarily, but the ball came out again to Gunn who lived up to his name by ramming home a shot against which our goal-keeper had not the slightest chance.

While Lorimer's went nearly mad, we bit our lips and wondered what the end would be.

'Vassall! Vassall! Vassall! Come along, Vassall!'

The juniors had joined voice. Now they were calling upon a hero to perform his wonders; formerly they had used up their lung-power in shouting him off the field.

The Tads' centre-forward responded to the cries by darting past Padmore, swerving by the left-back, and shooting with terrific force.

Another few inches, and Tads' would have equalized. As it was, the ball hit the upright with such force that it rebounded thirty feet.

We were having no luck—as this episode fully illustrated. A minute later the game was stopped, and when play proceeded Vassall, our main hope, could be seen hopping on one foot. He had been badly kicked.

Stimulated by the lead they had gained, Lorimer's swarmed to the attack again; their obvious intention was to smite while they had the opportunity. And as Tads and I watched them work in our goal-area, we both realized, I think, that another goal would make the issue safe—for them.

It was then that we saw a wonderful defence put up. Birtles was the one man in our team, now that Vassall was injured, and he rose fully to the occasion. The skipper was playing finely, it is true—he always did that —but the one man in the Tads' team who showed up head and shoulders above his fellows was Birtles. His dark head and somewhat heavy figure were everywhere.

Twice he saved what looked like certain goals. In the first case with the Tads' keeper out of goal, he dropped back and headed out a rasping shot from Padmore, and not many minutes afterwards, when Harptree had been hopelessly beaten again, he made a desperate spurt and overtaking the rival inside-left when the latter was about to shoot, charged him clean off the ball.

I took a look at Tads' face. The house-master had an expression which warmed the heart. No doubt he was thinking how thoroughly justified he had been in making that last effort to keep Birtles on the straight road.

The crowd "rose" at the left-back, and when half-time came his play was the general topic of conversation.

Tads beckoned Vassall over.

'How's the ankle?'

'Getting better now, sir, thank you—I say, isn't Birtles putting up a ripping game?'

Tads smiled. 'I'm glad I liked Vassall from the beginning,' he remarked to me; 'one likes to see one's judgment justified.'

After the re-start, the pace of the game became hotter than ever. Lorimer's were determined to keep their lead, while our fellows naturally were anxious to equalize.

The limelight became shifted—it flashed from Birtles to Vassall—and stayed on the centre-forward. With his ankle better, he became his old self—a flashing form in jersey and shorts.

Once again he came speeding down the centre, beating Padmore for possession. With the backs closing in on him, he sent well out to the right, and this time Geekie trapped the ball and went scampering away with that long-legged stride of his which was as effective as it was comical.

We saw the Lorimer's left-back go plunging across, and then two figures went to the turf together.

But up rose a scream from Tads'.

'*Corner!*'

A corner it was; and we watched with what the sensational lady novelist would call "bated breath", while Geekie did his well-known imitation of William Meredith.

The ball came curling across—we saw a head—Vassall's—leap upwards. But Lorimer's goalkeeper was on the alert, and with a hefty punch he got the ball clear.

Then—

'Stanhope!' rose the yell.

Tads' skipper had been hovering round. The ball came straight to his foot. Without hesitation he lunged at it.

'*Goal!*'

How the ball went clean through the ruck of players that were clustered in the goal mouth no one had the least idea. And the most startled and bewildered player of all was Lorimer's goalkeeper, judging by his expression.

But now the score was equal—that was the main thing. The Tads' team gathered round their skipper and nearly smothered him. Amongst those offering congratulations I noticed Birtles.

With the score 1-1, excitement rose higher still. Every kick was followed with strained and painful attention.

But, although frenzy ruled practically all the time, it remained for the last five minutes to bring the supreme thrill.

And this is how it happened. Once again Vassall fed Geekie. The ball was so truly passed that it might have gone to the outside-right on a string.

Geekie was now playing a storming game. He raced past his back, and centred low and true from near the corner-flag.

Directly they saw that their back was beaten, Lorimer's fled to the goal mouth. Here they surrounded the centre-forward whom they had every reason to fear.

But Vassall, racing shoulder to shoulder with Padmore, seemed to lift himself from the ground with both feet. One foot—his right—smote the ball, which fled at a tangent towards the goal.

Too late Lorimer's crowd shouted; the goalkeeper remained at his post near the left upright, while the ball flicked the opposite post—and glided gently into the net.

Only three minutes were left for play when the ball was kicked to the centre. And the Tads' defence prevailed throughout that brief period.

The victorious team trailed off the field, muddy, dog-tired but very content.

By some strange chance Stanhope, Birtles, and Vassall were together.

CHAPTER XXVIII

The Better Man

The Easter term was infinitely the most at Repington. Apart from football, there were boxing championships to be decided.

Now, the procedure was this: each house was supposed to supply a candidate in each of the three divisions—lights, middles, and heavies. Who should have the supreme honour of representing the shop at King's in the Public School Tourney was decided after due trial and approval by the gymnastic instructor and special committee of the masters, of which Tads was chairman.

Tads' House, so far as the general public was concerned, understood that Birtles would certainly be selected in the heavies. Birtles thought so himself. Hadn't he represented the house in the middles the year before, and been nearly selected to go to King's for the school?

Football was, of course, McPhail's chief passion. That was why it was not until the question of who should represent the house in the different boxing classes commenced to intrigue everyone at Tads' that he sought out Vassall.

'I say, Vassall,' he remarked with the candour of a privileged person, 'you were an ass to chuck your boxing with Benny Bennison. Murtrie,' (the gym instructor) 'is all right in a way, of course, but Bennison would knock spots off him. And if you had kept on, you would have stood a chance of being chosen for the house in the heavies.'

Vassall turned on his critic.

'That is the very reason I kept away from Bennison's place. I didn't want it to be said that I was getting lessons from a pro. But, of course,' he added hastily, as though anxious that even his friend should not misunderstand him, 'there isn't the least chance of my name going up.'

'There would have been if you hadn't chucked your lessons. Why, last term you were a perfect masterpiece considering the time you had been at the game. I'm going to speak to Stanhope—we want the best man, and I'm not certain that you wouldn't lick Birtles if you had the chance in a fair scrap.'

'I don't want to be pushed—'

But McPhail was gone. Once he had made up his mind about a matter he was not prepared to listen to any argument.

It happened that that same afternoon Tads was taking council with Murtrie.

The latter, naturally a pessimistic individual, was inclined to be optimistic for once.

'Between ourselves, sir, I don't think there's a heavy in the school better than Birtles,' he said. 'I had the gloves on with him to-day—and he was extra good.'

Tads adjusted his waistcoat.

'I don't know but what I may find a boy in my house better than Birtles, Murtrie.'

The gym instructor looked blank.

'Well, if you have, sir, I haven't set eyes on him yet.'

'I'll bring him along this afternoon,' replied the house-master.

Murtrie continued to look incredulous.

'The position is this,' said Tads; 'before I can make my final selection I want to see you box another boy in the house. Murtrie has just spoken highly of you, Birtles, but I happen to know that Vassall—'

'Vassall!' exclaimed Birtles, evidently thoroughly astonished.

'Vassall, I said,' returned the house-master.

'Now I hope you know me well enough, Birtles, to believe that I have no more personal preference for Vassall than I have for you. You have lately proved yourself a good sportsman, and I know that you are keen on representing the house in the heavies. But I must choose the best boy—you will admit that, of course?'

'Yes, sir.' Birtles looked bewildered. 'But Vassall—I did not know he was keen on boxing. If I had known—' He broke off. What he had in his mind to say was that if he had known his old enemy had had any pretensions to boxing he would have challenged him to a stand-up fight long before. It was only the fact that he felt the school would have imagined he had taken advantage of Vassall that had kept his hands off him last term. Only Birtles himself knew what a sacrifice it had meant for him to ignore challenge which Vassall had once thrown out to fight on the spot on a certain occasion.

'What do you propose then, sir?' he asked. There was an eagerness in his tone which Tads did not fail to remark.

'What I propose is that you and Vassall shall box three rounds in the gym to decide which is the better boy to represent the house in the heavies. I have not mentioned the subject to Vassall, but I have no doubt that he will agree.'

'And of course I will, sir!' Although his feelings towards Vassall had undergone a change, yet he felt that a fight of some sort had been inevitable between them ever since the other had come to Repington, and this was a splendid opportunity. Besides, it was necessary for him to demonstrate his unassailable right to be the best heavy in the house.

'Very well—I knew you would not have any objection,' concluded the house-master. 'I will arrange it as soon as possible.'

The news hit the house with dramatic force; there was a picturesque touch about it which was irresistible.

Tads himself came to me with the news that Vassall had agreed to box three rounds with Birtles to decide who was the better man.

'I am afraid the house is so keen on this test that everyone will want to be in the gym when it comes off, Watney,' he said, with that understanding smile of his.

'Of course, sir,' I replied, 'everyone in the house is frightfully keen in the circumstances,' looking him straight in the face, 'who wouldn't be?'

He smiled. 'You seem to know what was in my mind, Watney, when I proposed this affair.'

'I think I do, sir. Aren't you hoping that, after the hard fight which is sure to result, Vassall and Birtles may become friends?'

He put a hand heavily on my shoulder.

'That is what I am hoping, Watney; I do not know if we can expect that it will happen—but it is my hope and wish.'

Need I say that the gym was crowded? In the miraculously quick way in which news of this vital character always travels, the whole school had got to hear of the affair. Fellows were crushing and crowding desperately anxious to get a squint.

I got a seat all right—Tads saw to that. So did McPhail, Stanhope, and all the rest of our little colony. After all this was our right, and the fellows from the other houses were really outsiders.

'This fellow Vassall used to be a frightful funk-shy at footer, didn't he?' a chap from Canaver's shot up at me.

'Wait and see,' I replied.

Vassall, when he showed up, was looking pale and a trifle under the weather. Then I remembered that he had had a beastly cold. But there was no sign of any funk; he was strung up, certainly—who wouldn't have been?—but he always had that expression before a football match. It was the old, familiar greyhound-fretting-at-its-leash business: nothing in it, except keenness to begin.

He was warmly received, and the cheers must have been appreciated, for he commenced flushing and looking happier at once.

Then came Birtles—and the applause was deafening. The noise evidently took Birtles by surprise. He looked round with a surprised and curious smile as though he were asking: Why the sudden change? Of course, his return to the football team had gained him friends where before he had enemies, but he had never been a really popular fellow in the house.

McPhail nudged my elbow.

'They're cheering more for the prospect of the scrap than because of Birtles,' he said, and I believe he was right.

I must have told my tale badly if you cannot visualize the scene as the signal was given for the first round to commence. To me it seemed that every event in which these two had been concerned had but led up to this meeting.

Those who expected Birtles to be openly gloating now that the chance had come for which in the old days he must so often have longed, were disappointed. True, there was a hint of joyous satisfaction in his eyes, while a grim smile played about his lips—but that was all. Perhaps he knew that he would require all his powers as a fighter in the coming bout; perhaps a new and totally unexpected respect for his opponent had sprung up within him. Who could say?

Stripped, the two showed distinct differences, Vassall being a trifle longer in the reach and taller than Birtles, who had the advantage in muscular development, and a frame that looked as though it would stand more punishment than the fair-skinned body of Vassall.

Birtles, true to his nature, carried the fight to his man at once. He almost leapt at Vassall to deliver the first blow. But Vassall was "away," gliding out of danger with a sure-footed grace that brought the cheers swinging up to the roof.

Again Birtles rushed, and it seemed to me that Vassall must go down before that thundering assault.

But, although he sustained a thump on the side of the head—if he had not been quick on his feet that swish would have landed clean on the "point"—he weathered the storm successfully, and then began to fight back. He did not show the same passionate ardour as his opponent, but he contrived to draw blood with a left hook to the mouth, and by the end of the round it seemed to me that the honours were easy, for in his rally he had gathered as many points as Birtles. Neither was unscathed, however, as they went to their corners.

142

In the second round Birtles pursued the same tactics. He seemed as strong as a bull, and no matter how many times his moves were countered, he was back again at the attack, hammering away with both glove So furious was this second assault that Vassall was forced to remain on the defensive; and if he had not kept cool and steady he would have been beaten to the floor by the sheer impetuosity of his rival. Twice he had to seek refuge on the ropes, but each time he extricated himself from what appeared a forlorn position by sheer dexterity. On both occasions cheers went up at his staving off of defeat, for he carried more votes than Birtles. Still the fact remained that the second round was Birtles's.

The knowledge—for he must have known it—did not appear to worry him unduly as he sat in his corner. He seemed in better shape than Birtles, for the latter was breathing heavily. The two still presented a vivid contrast. Vassall appeared to regard the business as pleasant sort of relaxation, but Birtles's expression registered grim determination. He was out to win every fibre of his being.

Yet, to the general surprise, it was Vassall who scored first in that decisive third round. With an immaculately straight left, he brought Birtles up with a snort of mingled surprise and vexation, when his opponent, following out his plan of campaign, rushed into attack again.

The boxing from this point became dazzling in its quickness and dexterity. Vassall now was not content to keep on the defensive; with hurricane velocity, he launched an attack himself. Birtles, nothing loath, "wired in," and we saw the two old enemies banging away at each other with right good will.

It was not merely hefty slogging: both fellows proved that they could box with skill and judgment. Much of the work they did was very fine.

There could have been only a minute to go, when Vassall almost imperceptibly commenced to force the pace. Up till this point honours in this final round were so even that it would have required a very expert referee indeed to have given a decision. But now foot by foot Birtles was being forced steadily back to the ropes.

A quick feint—and Vassall's left had rattled home against Birtles's heart. There must have been a tremendous amount of power behind the blow, for he sagged against the ropes, and with one arm weakly guarding his face, he looked like a beaten gladiator at bay.

'Vassall! Vassall!' rose the cry.

But the blow which would have finished it was never delivered. Vassall, too, appeared at the end of his tether; the limit of his endurance seemed to have been reached. Anyway, when the bell went, he was still standing over his opponent, but he had not struck him again.

No decision was announced, but it seemed the general opinion that a draw could be the only possible result. We worked it out as follows:—the first round honours were level; Birtles had gained the second round, and Vassall the third. If he had only taken advantage of the opening he had made for himself at the end—but he hadn't, and so he would have to be content with a draw.

But a draw meant that the selectors would be faced with the same problem. The fight had not solved the question of who should represent the house in the heavies.

D 484

"VASSALL! VASSALL!" ROSE THE CRY

CHAPTER XXIX

The Finish of the Feud

After banging once loudly, Birtles burst into the study. 'Do you think I'm the sort to take a favour from you, Vassall—after what has happened?' he demanded angrily.

Before that day Vassall might have resented the tone. His face would probably have flushed, and he would have been on his quiet dignity at once.

'Thanks for an awfully good scrap, Birtles,' he said calmly; 'I say, won't you sit down? Now, what's all this about a favour? I haven't done you any favour.'

Birtles stared, and as he looked the belligerent look died out of his face.

'Haven't you just told Tads that you won't represent the house in the heavies?'

'Certainly. I'm giving way to a better man. You'd lick me into a cocked hat over a long distance, Birtles. You've got better staying power, and more of the real fighting instinct.' He put his hand up to a lumpy ear. 'I don't think I shall be able to hear again this side for a week,' he added.

Birtles leaned forward in his chair.

'What made you stop that punch in the last round?' he demanded; 'you know as well as I do that you had me absolutely at your mercy in the last minute—and yet it was only a touch that I got. They said it was a draw—but you could have beaten me sick if you wanted to. My guard was down and as I say you had me—well, where you wanted me. Don't think I mind saying it,' he continued challengingly; 'we've never been friends, but I hope to goodness I can give credit to a man—even if I don't like him.'

'I boxed as well as I knew how, Birtles,' replied the other, 'and here's something I have wanted to tell you for some time. I had lessons from a pro. Not this term—last term—I don't know if it was quite fair.'

146

Birtles stared again. His expression seemed to intimate that he couldn't quite make this chap out.

'What about it? A fellow can't expect to know how to box unless he has lessons of some sort, can he? My father used to engage a pro down at Merrywood for me, just because I didn't think over-much of Murtrie as an instructor. Why shouldn't you have had lessons from a pro?'

Vassall seemed to find this question awkward to answer and so he kept silent.

'It's quite understood that you're not to represent Tads' in the heavies then?' persisted Birtles; 'that's what I came along for—that, and another thing, which I'll mention later.'

'No—I'm not going to represent Tads'. I already explained why, Birtles. Oh, I'm not doing you a favour: I'm just telling you the truth when O say that you've proved the better man.'

'Rot!'

'Truth! And I'm keener on football than boxing, as a matter of fact. Boxing is only a side-line with me. I only took it up to help me stop funking at football.'

'But Tads will be sure to pick you.'

'He won't. I have already told him what I'm trying to din into your thick head—that I shouldn't have a chance with you over a distance.'

'But I'm not going to have it—I shall see Tads for myself!' exploded Birtles.

'What's all this clamour about?' asked the house-master, unexpectedly entering the study. 'You two aren't having a second fight, are you?'

'It has nearly come to that, sir,' smiled back Vassall; 'Birtles is demanding that I shall offer myself up as a sacrifice by representing Tads' in the heavies boxing when,' looking at the master straight in the eyes, 'in the first place I know I shall not be chosen, and secondly when I'm not the better man. Birtles wants convincing, sir—I know you will convince him.'

Tads returned the look which he had been given, and then touched Birtles on the shoulder.

'You have been chosen for the heavies—and Murtrie and I both think that you will go to King's, Birtles,' he said. He snatched a look at his watch; 'I'll be getting along,' he added quickly, and left the two alone.

Birtles breathed deeply.

'When you first came to the shop I did a pretty rotten thing,' he said; 'I ragged your study and pinned a card on you. I want to say—'

He broke off to watch Vassall go to a cupboard and unlock it.

147

'That's the thing, isn't it?' Vassall held a card on which were rudely printed in large letters the words:

I AM A FUNK.

'Yes, that's the thing,' concurred Birtles.

'At one time I thought of giving it back to you, Birtles.'

The other gulped.

'I'll take it back,' he said quickly; and forthwith commenced to tear it to pieces.

'I'm sorry,' he added, walking to the door.

With his hand on the knob, he stopped. Gulping again, he returned.

'I know my people and your mother will never hit it —they're not the same class—but—if—you—like—'

'I shall be jolly glad to be a pal of yours, Birtles, cut in Vassall, and held out his hand.

The other clasped it warmly.

CHAPTER XXX

The Helping Hand

'What I want to know, Watney, is whether this David-and-Jonathan business would have come off, if Vassall had plunked the fellow as he ought to have done when he had him lying across the ropes?'

'What's the good of speculating, you young ass?' I replied; 'it's a good thing for the house, isn't it, that Birtles and Vassall are now friends?'

'Oh, quite—quite,' Stanhope's fag muttered, and walked away, looking subdued and thoughtful. My impression was that McPhail was suffering from the pangs of the green god, Jealousy. He had enjoyed the company of Vassall almost exclusively since the latter had been at the shop, and now that Birtles and Vassall were as close friends as before they had been bitter enemies, McPhail suffered in his soul. At least, that was my impression.

But McPhail need not have feared that he was going to be left out in the cold. The day after the reconciliation, Vassall, who was walking across to the gym with Birtles, espied Stanhope's fag.

'Mac!' he shouted.

McPhail came over, a question in his eyes. As a matter of fact, he *was* a trifle fed-up with this David-and-Jonathan business. Being decent to a chap who had proved that, deep down within him, there was some crude gold, was one thing, but Vassall falling on his foe's neck was something out of an entirely different basket, in his opinion, as he had so often muttered to himself.

'Hullo, Vassall,' he said, regarding Birtles out of the corner of his eye.

'Birtles wants us to train him for King's, Mac,' was the surprising remark Vassall made; 'of course, as we know, he's already the best heavy in the house, but we want him to be the best heavy in the shop. Then we shan't have much fear of what may happen at King's.'

McPhail brightened. After all Birtles had redeemed his character somewhat, and he was a Tads' man.

'If I can do anything,' he offered.

149

'You can do a lot,' said Birtles quickly; 'you trained Vassall in his football, he tells me, and—'

'The first thing to do, in my opinion,' broke in the fag, who had a suspicion that Birtles, in his reformed character, might be getting a trifle "mushy," is to go and see Benny Bennison—he will be the proper lad for the job.'

The ex-pugilist listened attentively while Vassall did the necessary talking.

'And you say he's better than you, Mr. Vassall—better than you were back along when you came to me for lessons regular?'

'Much better, Bennison. He hits harder—'

'Rot!' ejaculated Birtles.

'He hits harder, and can go a greater distance, I may be a trifle faster—'

'That's what I want—principally, I mean, broke in Birtles. 'As a matter of fact Vassall should be to King's, because he's really the better man—he proved it in a scrap we had recently in the gym—but he says he won't go, and so there's an end to it. But he's been decent enough to promise to spar with me—to give me quickness. It's speed I want—I know that.'

'You'd better put the gloves on, gen'l'men,' said Benny; 'then I can form an opinion for myself.'

The memory of other days came back to both Vassall and McPhail as the gloves were produced and put on. What a quaint but jolly old world it was, after all, reflected Vassall—he had learned boxing to help cure himself of being a funk, and was now finding it useful in giving a helping hand to a chap he had never thought he could face without enmity. And for the good of Tads'!

Three quick rounds were boxed under the eagle eye of Benny Bennison who, hopping round the contestants, kept giving sage advice something after this fashion: 'Now, Mr. Vassall—ah! there's nothing beats the straight left! It's won all the honours in the world... A little quicker with that right, Mr. Birtles, and it'll be a winner... keep your guard well up... now, step in, feint with the left—a real smart right, Mr. Birtles, and I can make it better yet if you place yourself in my hands. I don't want to boast, but if I can't get you ready for King's, no one can!'

McPhail looked at the scene with appraising eyes. Nothing could be hidden from the keenest mind in Repington.

He remembered how Vassall had allowed Birtles to escape when he had him on the ropes in the last round of the gym fight—and he had a suspicion now that Vassall could have guarded that wicked right smash which had excited Benny Bennison's admiration. He did not know that

Vassall was altogether playing the game from the house point of view in urging his old enemy to go to King's, when he himself might have been able to put up a better show; but if he did not agree with the decision he admired the spirit that prompted this sacrifice. And, anyway, the fellow was in Tads'. Moreover, he had so much confidence in Bennison—witness what he had done for Vassall in the early days—that he told his sporting conscience to be quiet whilst he got on with the job.

'Well, Bennison?' he queried, taking the ex-pugilist on one side, 'what is your candid opinion? In a way I am responsible for this fellow Birtles, and I want to know what you really think. Can you make him good enough?'

'I can, Mr. McPhail; I can, sir!'

'Good enough!' replied McPhail, his mind relieved. 'I'll see to things my end.'

He kept his word. No regular trainer of a boxer training for a world's championship could have done more than McPhail did. He guarded his charge as though he were a Derby favourite. In addition to the usual football training, he took Birtles for long road-runs (no, McPhail did not run himself, he rode a cycle), disciplined him severely in the matter of food, and escorted him personally to Bennison's Boxing Academy each day.

If Birtles was amused he never showed it. As a matter of fact this complex personality was full of gratitude. McPhail—from whom nothing was hidden—realized this. But he would have acted in exactly the same way if he hadn't.

Boxing daily with Vassall, Tads' hope rapidly became quicker in his work, and a week before King's, Benny Bennison professed himself to be entirely satisfied.

And when they heard this it was doubtful which face—Vassall's, McPhail's, or Birtles's—showed the most satisfaction.

'I'll try not to let any of you down,' said Birtles, as he took off his gloves.

CHAPTER XXXI

The Conqueror at King's

I must explain King's. When the authorities in 1921 reluctantly abandoned the Public Schools Boxing Championships[6] at the Queen's Avenue Gymnasium, Aldershot, much regret was expressed. Certain schools with strong sporting traditions held a meeting at which it was resolved to continue the Boxing Championships. King's Gymnasium, London, was the selected venue. This year the entries promised to be more numerous than ever, and consequently the competition to be keener.

It was a merry party of us that travelled up from the shop. Birtles by this time had been freely and frankly accepted as one of us, had been given "the freedom of the City," to use McPhail's characteristic phrase and we all wished fervently for his success. The boy had changed completely, and his attitude proved that his only desire now was to bring credit to the house and to the shop rather than luxuriate in glory himself.

Benny Bennison was included in our party. He had pleaded as a special favour to come with us, and to help second Birtles. Tads, to whom the request had been made, had readily given the necessary permission. Like a true sportsman he dismissed any thought that the thing might be slightly irregular.

We found King's filling rapidly when we arrived. The critics can say what they like about England going to the dogs, but there was not much evidence to that effect in witnessing a huge building like King's becoming crammed by representatives of all classes of society to watch a sport which above everything else is typically British. This crowd had not been drawn there by the thrilling prospect of seeing two world-famous fistic

---

[6] The annual Boxing, Fencing, and Gymnastic Competition did actually take place at the Army's Queen's Road Gymnasium, in Aldershot - it featured in an early P.G. Wodehouse novel *The Pothunters*.

stars; they had not been lured by columns of newspaper "gush," which is becoming nauseating, especially when—as is so frequently obvious—the writers evidently do not know their subject; no, this crowd was one of genuine sportsmen and sportswomen who had gathered in the best interests of perhaps the finest game ever known.

Of course, a great many relatives had come. Birtles's *père* and *mère* were amongst these. They greeted their son with enthusiasm. From somewhere Birtles had acquired an "air"; he introduced us all with a charm that was as surprising as it was unexpected.

After that he went away, accompanied by McPhail and Vassall. He looked anxious, but not nervous. Benny Bennison had not yet arrived—he had been forced to keep a business appointment which had detained him—but Birtles found his two friends company enough.

He was feeling as he had never felt before: the time approaching was in the nature of a test. Would he be man enough to meet it? He had to win the heavies not only for Tads' but for the shop. In that way, he felt, he could do penance and give recompense for being such an outsider in days that were gone—but only in that way.

He had to justify himself: that was his view. In his heart he knew that Vassall had given way to him, had sacrificed his own claims. Vassall should have been putting on the gloves that day for Tads' honour. And, because he stood in Vassall's place, because he was in a measure Vassall's deputy, he had to do his more than his best—and more than his best. He had to rise to heights that day which he had never before scaled.

It was curious that he thought first of his comrades and then of his people. Prior to that understanding with Vassall the order would have been reversed—his first consideration would have been the glorification and the triumphing of the name of Birtles—what would he have cared for all the rotten snobs by whom he had been surrounded? Hang them, and the house—and the school!

Wondering at the change which had come over him, Birtles knew that he had found his soul.

'By Jove! they've started!' said McPhail.

'I must be off, I suppose, then,' remarked Birtles, and just then a familiar figure came up to the group of Repingtonians. It was Benny Bennison.

'I think you had better be thinking of getting ready, Mr. Birtles.'

'Righto, Bennison!' He rose, and with a nod to the two walked away.

'Decent chap!' chirped McPhail.

'White man!' said Vassall.

Apart from possibly the relatives who had a special interest in watching, the early bouts between feathers and light weights proved somewhat uninteresting. It was the heavies that the majority of the spectators were so anxious to see.

A storm of applause greeted the first pair—Blundell of Sandburn, and Merrick of Clifden. Well-built boys both, this bout promised some fine sport.

It was not until the third round, however, that any really decent boxing was seen, for now that the great moment had arrived, both contestants failed to do themselves justice. They boxed wildly and with little regard to the rules and science which no doubt had been so carefully drilled into them by their instructors.

In the third round, however, warmed to their work and accustomed to their surroundings, they both boxed well.

Birtles, changed, watched attentively. He was "on" next, so he had been told. In the dressing-rooms he had caught sight of his first opponent —a gangling, awkward-looking youth from Ashfield—a school that has turned out some first-rate boxers to send up to the university.

As the bout he had been watching came to an end, with the winner the Clifden boy, a sudden wave of nausea passed through Birtles. It was not fear of being hurt but fear of not doing himself justice, and thus bitterly disappointing all those who were decent enough to wish him well.

He felt as though all the sensibility had momentarily left him; his head was swimming, the figures in the ring went round and round.

'Your turn, Mr. Birtles,' said a voice.

It was the fact of looking into the steady grey eyes of Benny Bennison that pulled him together. A wave of some revivifying force that gave him back his poise passed from Bennison to him. His head ceased to swim, his eyesight became normal, as, greeted by a wild burst of applause, he ducked quickly under the ropes of the ring.

The referee said in a loud voice:

'S. M. Berriman, Ashfield, boxes J. D. Birtles, Repington.'

'Go careful for the first round, Mr. Birtles. He looks awkward, but you can never tell. Get his measure in the first round—and then you'll know where you are and how you stand.'

'Time!'

Those who watched, their nerves a-throb, and their hearts beating wildly, saw Birtles shake his head before darting from his corner to clasp hands with his opponent.

The latter proved quite as awkward as he looked. Evidently believing in early finishes, he rushed more or less blindly at Birtles, and, if the Repington representative had not shaken off the mental lethargy by which he had been attacked a few minutes before, he must have succumbed to this whirlwind, if clumsy, assault.

But the lessons of self-control which Benny Bennison had taken so much trouble to instil into him during the practice bouts had their effect. A voice was murmuring to Birtles: 'Keep cool—guard well up—take it steady—wear him down!'

He side-stepped neatly as the other came thundering in, feinted with his right and pumped home his left.

The blow landed nicely on the jaw, rocking the impetuous one.

The small mental voice which had spoken to him before now sent Birtles another message.

'Here's your chance!' it said.

Indeed, it seemed so, for the other boy was floundering. Stepping close, the Repington representative swung his right with cool but deadly precision. Birtles felt a stab of pain shoot through his hand before he watched to his intense surprise his opponent fall heavily to the floor of the ring.

A volley of frenzied cheers broke out, but Birtles stood stupefied. He could not realize that he had won the first bout—the bout which he had dreaded most of all, and which he had been afraid he would not survive.

It had been so easy—once he had gripped himself, and had refused to be flustered by that first unnerving attack of his opponent.

Almost angrily Birtles looked at the boy who was still on the floor. Why didn't he get up and fight? He himself, now that he had started, wanted to fight—to keep on fighting. What was the use in getting into a ring at all if you didn't fight?

'Ten!' said the referee, and made a signal. The defeated boy's seconds ducked beneath the ropes, and dragged the vanquished away. The referee pointed to Birtles, and the cheering broke out like a hurricane.

Before he could quite realize it was over, Birtles found people thumping him on the back.

'Nice work, B.!' commented McPhail; 'keep that right in working order and you ought to bring home the bacon. What do you say, Bennison?'

'I'm very pleased with you, Mr. Birtles,' replied the ex-pugilist.

A little success is a wonderful tonic. Birtles, as he sat with his friends after resuming his coat, felt that life was worth living.

Then he had a misgiving. This low-browed Jewish-looking boy, wearing the Overbury scarlet and black on his boxing vest, was hitting his opponent all over the ring. He had attacked from the first bell, and was still attacking. Wonderfully light on his feet, he smashed home blows from all angles. Each glove carried danger, as was seen when, after giving more ground, the St. George's boy he was fighting parried a vicious left only to be knocked flat by a murderous right-hand jab that apparently did not travel more than twelve inches.

Bennett of St. George's went down—and stayed down.

'H'm!' McPhail muttered, 'I don't like the look of that slaughterer one little bit. He's going to disturb my night's rest if he isn't careful.'

On his right he could see Benny Bennison bending towards Birtles and speaking earnestly.

'Good old Bennison!' he said to Vassall, 'pull B. through!'

Vassall nodded. But his secret fear was that the Overbury fighting-machine would prove too fast for Birtles to withstand successfully for three whole rounds.

What Bennison had said to his charge was this: 'You must keep your nerve! You showed you can keep it in the last bout—but you must not let go of it for a moment! This Gunter fellow can fight—he's a natural fighter —and will probably go through to the final. It's as likely as not that you will meet him there. It'll be a grand scrap if you do—but you must keep your nerve!'

And, to the open rejoicing of all his friends, Birtles kept his nerve so well that he went clean through to the final. But—and it was a big But— so did Gunter, the hurricane smasher from Overbury.

One could have heard a pin drop when the referee called:

'Final, heavy-weights,' and then:

'A. C. Gunter, Overbury.' A roar of applause, during which Gunter smiled.

No doubt he meant it for a pleasant smile, but to the Repington crowd it appeared highly sinister.

'Perhaps it's the shape of his face—after all he can't help his face!' said McPhail.

'J. D. Birtles, Repington,' finished the referee.

The noise that had gone before was a mere zephyr compared to a gale. I saw Birtles's strong, rugged face twitch as the cheers beat about him. Then came that expression which we of Repington had learned to know so well.

It was a moment of dramatic tension. On either side of the ring were the two boys who were about to battle for the greatest honour in public school boxing. Both had their instructors bending over them whispering their last words of advice and caution. Like two greyhounds straining to be off they waited—

'Box him! Do you hear, box him!' those near enough heard Bennison say in a strained, hoarse voice.

156

Birtles nodded, signifying that he heard and understood. But in that moment his eye caught the smile of Vassall who was seated near the ringside. The smile told him to be of good cheer.

'Time!' called the referee.

Birtles rose at the summons. But he was allowing his mind to wander. That smile of Vassall's had conjured up a good many memories.

The result of this momentary distraction was that before he could properly prepare himself after shaking hands with his opponent, the latter was on him, ramming home blows with both fists.

A gasp of horror came from the Repington contingent. What was Birtles thinking about? What was the matter with the man?

Jammed into a corner, Birtles too late realized his mistake. He covered up, receiving smashing blows on both arms. He did not mind the stings; better receive them on his arms than on more vital spots.

A sense of thankfulness came that he was still on his feet; that he was not already beaten—that he still had a chance. Manoeuvring swiftly, he extricated himself somewhat.

Gunter then made his mistake. Chagrined that he could not penetrate the other's guard, although he had outwitted him in that first thrilling minute of the fight, he threw caution aside and went all out for the final blow which would give him victory.

Now was Birtles's chance. He realized it, getting home a left jab that sent Gunter staggering back into the centre of the ring.

Birtles quickly followed. Now he had all the ring in which to fight. He was out of danger. What a fool he had been ever to get into it!

Making a curious noise that might have been a sniff of contempt, Gunter renewed the assault. With all the skill in defence that he had gained from Bennison, Birtles began wondering whether the fellow had a dozen fists instead of the customary two. Blows continued to rain upon him—some, he knew, might well have knocked him out if he had been the least bit unlucky.

This was the most gruelling time he had ever experienced since he had put on boxing gloves in earnest: it was worse—or seemed so—than boxing with Bennison himself, even when the pugilist let himself "go."

He knew he mustn't think of Bennison; all he had to think about was the man before him, this human whirlwind who was trying to batter the sense out of him. As though to remind him forcibly of the fact came a stinging swing on the side of the head which caused him to reel.

In trying to regain his balance he slipped, crashing to the floor.

'Stand back!'

He heard the sharp command of the referee and looked up into the hard face of his opponent. Was this fellow Gunter going to lick him? Was he going to allow himself to be licked? He choked at the thought.

Bennison had taught him the value of waiting until the referee had counted "8" and when the number left the official's lips he rose. The sudden hush that had fallen over the crowd became then an uproarious clamour.

The few seconds' rest had done him good. And, curiously enough, the blow on the head had seemed to clear his brain. Dogged he had been before, but now he was cool and calculating.

So it was that when the human avalanche hurled himself forward once again, he was met by a very business-like left that did not improve the shape of his already not over-elegant nose. It was a real boxer's left, and brought tears of joy to Benny Bennison's puckered eyes.

Gunter seemed so surprised at being hit that momentarily he wavered. And then the mischief was done, for Birtles, slouching forward with that somewhat awkward shuffle of his, planted right and left in quick succession into his opponent's ribs.

Gunter grunted, and swung a haymaker right. Had it landed the fight would have ended.

But Birtles had not presumed upon his unexpected good fortune. He was "away," and the desperate effort wasted its wickedness upon the empty air.

'Now!' called a voice.

Instantly Birtles realized that fortune had given him a second chance. In two strides he was within hitting distance of the foe who was staggering through the force of the wasted blow.

A clean sweet right it was—and Gunter dropped.

Then the bell went.

'You've won, lad!' Bennison was elatedly fussing over his pupil, but Birtles was staring across the ring. In mercy he had not put all his weight behind the blow. At the time he felt he had been wrong—and now he was convinced. For Gunter, instead of being "out," had revived; although his eyes lacked lustre he was talking to his seconds.

'Well, I'm jiggered!' exclaimed Bennison: 'I thought you had outed him.'

Birtles did not reply. His cup was full. This was the first time he had ever shown mercy to a foe—and the act had recoiled upon him. His teeth were clenched at the call of "Time!"

The second round of the final heavies at King's that year went down to history. Those who care to read about it in detail may look up the *Sportsman* for that date.

Gunter, seemingly but little affected by the blow which had floored him, and anxious to make amends, re-started his storming tactics directly he left his corner. With a bound he was across the ring and working at his blacksmith's trade once more. The fellow seemed made of steel and whipcord.

He was resolutely met. Birtles had decided there should be no retreating in this round. He was willing to take all that the other could give him, and return the blows with interest.

The crowd rose to their feet, for here was a FIGHT, not a boxing match. At the end of the round it would have been difficult to say who had scored the more points. As a matter of fact the referee had given them equal marks.

'You were a bit too impetuous, sir, if you don't mind me mentioning it!'

Bennison had watched the whole of the round with his heart in his mouth.

'You'll see in the next round!' was the surprising reply.

The crowd saw as well as Bennison. From the start Birtles forced the pace. He was acting upon a deliberate plan of campaign. He had gauged the physical capacity of his foe. Vassall had been a shrewd judge when he said that his old enemy was a good man over three rounds. At the end of that uproarious rip-snorting second round Birtles had felt that Gunter had had about enough. Now, then, was the time to apply the finishing touch.

It was applied with a flash of boxing genius: the two met in the centre of the ring, Gunter still grimly determined, but with much of the audacious fire beaten out of him; Birtles more sure and confident than he had felt since the fight began.

A cool, almost insolent feint with the left, and Gunter dodged sideways—only to crash into a right that carried every ounce of strength that Birtles had in his sturdy body.

There was no mistake this time. Gunter went down —and he stayed down. He was still down after the referee had come to the fateful "Ten!"

And then the Conqueror of King's was received into the safe custody of his friends.

CHAPTER XXXII

Mud and Glory

We passed from excitement to excitement. The air at Repington seemed charged with electricity these days.

The dearest hopes of Tads' had been realized: when the last week of the term came it was known that Canaver's and Tads' would take the field in the all-important match that was to decide the destination of the Corinthians' Cup.

'By Jove, Dot-and-Carry, it's difficult to realize it is true!' said Stanhope to me on the night before the game.

'It's true enough—and to-morrow at tea-time you'll be holding that blessed cup in your hands, old son!' I replied. The wish was more than father to the thought, of course.

Then the crowd burst into the study, and I had to listen instead of talk. For was I not a mere looker-on, instead of a chosen battler?

I am trying hard to keep a steady pen. But it is difficult to do so. Those who have followed my humble tale so far know all that hung on the result of our match with Canaver's. For one thing it meant that Stanhope — the finest skipper that even Tads' had ever had — would leave us with a contented mind; for another, victory to us meant the revival of an ancient and honourable tradition; we had been cock house at football before; in being so again we should maintain our record and keep free of stain our sporting standard.

Public opinion was against us—against the chance of our winning, I mean. We had merely scrambled to the final honour; Canaver's, on the other hand, had marched triumphantly towards their goal. They were a splendid team, strong if not brilliant in every department.

Yet we had Vassall: it was on the former funk-shy that we were building our faith.

'Vassall!'

As inspiring as an ancient call to arms, the name rang out. We shouted it from every part of the ground. Voices flung it fiercely forth as a challenge. By my side McPhail was repeating it softly as though he were saying a prayer.

In the centre of the field, the slim, supple-limbed boy answered the call by snapping up the pass which had been thrust through to him. He swerved past the plunging Canaver's half-back, and was away down the middle like the wind—the thunderous acclaim throbbing in his ears; mad but merry music.

As the opposing right-back challenged him, he wheeled with the deft grace a skilled skater shows on ice, and, without losing control of the ball, cut inwards.

'Vassall!' We shouted it again.

Sounding louder and louder like some mighty, majestic chant the name swelled. Now it had a note of appeal, almost of anguish. If he should bungle this chance—!'

He could see the Canaver's goalkeeper shaping himself for the shot he knew was coming, and in that moment we felt the fate of our house being weighed in the balance.

Nudging the ball on, he raised his foot—that already-famous left foot of his which had scored so many fine goals that season. But the goalkeeper, all his wits about him, had narrowed the angle at which he could shoot.

As quick as a flash, the ball sped forward—but we saw that Vassall had passed to a comrade instead of shooting himself. He had conquered the momentary temptation to finish off his own work. And how dire must that temptation have been!

Sprinting like a greyhound, Geekie, who had come inside, took the ball in his stride; ran two paces, and then fired at the far corner of the net. At such a range the shot was unstoppable. What was more, the manoeuvre had been so quickly planned that the goal-keeper was unprepared; he could only stand bewildered and helpless as the ball whistled past him.

First blood to Tads'!

Dare we regard this as an omen? Within three minutes of the start we had scored—could we maintain this advantage?

Cheers soon changed to groans. Perhaps Harptree was not to blame, but the fact remained that he slipped on the wet and treacherous turf—it was a vile day—and let in the Canaver's outside-left.

This fellow had a born footballer's brain. He ran on until he had lured Birtles to tackle him, and then slipped the ball across the goal mouth. Birtles made a desperate effort to intercept the pass, but he was too late.

With only the goalkeeper to beat, Matthews, the inside-right, took careful aim—and the ball was in the net.

Equality!

The pace was terrific—so fast that it could not possibly last. With one goal each to their credit both teams started to try to wear the other down.

We saw a vivid contrast in styles: Canaver's, now that they had recovered from their first blinding repulse, played with almost calm surety as though they were certain of final victory. Tads', a team that in some measure was one composed of makeshifts, were almost too eager—fretful, in a way, because of their anxiety, and desperate. There is always drama in football, but it was intensified on this dull, grey March afternoon.

The early thrusts and parries had given promise of tremendous happenings, and, although Canaver's looked the more confident team, we of Tads' still had high hopes.

This was the last game dear old Stanhope would play at the shop, and it was plain that he was not sparing himself. Time after time he went to the assistance of his wing halves when they were in trouble; time and again he turned defence into attack by tackling with hard but clean vigour and then urging his forwards to the attack once more.

But in this relentless encounter one man, however hard he worked, was powerless to stem a tide—and the tide seemed definitely set in Canaver's favour. At the end of the first quarter of an hour the opposition gradually commenced to exert its superiority. The backs took up an advanced position: strong kickers both, and unsparing tacklers to boot, they put plenty of power behind their clearances, so that their forwards, keeping well up on our backs, had many opportunities.

This change of tactics proved the weakness of our right-back. Harptree became flustered—how we missed Jenkins!—and Birtles had to strive like a superman to ward off disaster.

By really wonderful play he contrived, with the help of the goalkeeper, to prevent any further score, his intuition and positional play being alike splendid. The ball seemed to come to his head or foot by instinct.

It was from one of his clearances that Bridges at inside-left got possession and, dribbling a few yards, flicked inside to Vassall. The latter fired at once out to the right-wing. Geekie got the ball under instant control, and sped onwards. Tackled near the corner-flag, he swung round in his tracks and centred with his left foot.

Now was the time for us to catch our breath, gripped by suspense! The ball floated over the goal mouth. We could see Vassall leap upwards.

'Hard luck, Vassall!' called our legions.

Canaver's chap in goal had just got his fingers to the ball which was curling beneath the bar in the top right-hand corner, stayed it in some wonderful fashion, punched it partially clear, and then one of the backs completed the clearance, and we had to commence hoping all over again!

The pace continued bewildering. It was a fine tribute to the zealous training of both teams. For half an hour not one of the players spared a yard. It was to the last gasp all the time.

Of course, it could not last; something was bound to crack. To our delighted surprise it was Canaver's, not ourselves, who hoisted the first signals of distress. If only they had once achieved the lead anything might have happened, for then their confidence would have allowed them to run riot.

But solid grit had met collective brilliance—and had checkmated it. Apart from Vassall, Stanhope, Brittle, and Bridges, ours, as I have said before, was to a certain extent a makeshift team—we had had to build in some cases with indifferent material.

Yet it served: when Canaver's found that however much our defence floundered on the right, they could not break through again, they changed their tactics. They cut out the suspicion of cool superiority and over elaboration, and settled down to serious business.

Yet still the Tads' fort held.

It was at the end of that thrilling if gruelling first half an hour that Tads', answering their skipper's exhortation, commenced to give the first sign that they could outlast the opposition. Once again Bridges secured and with Vassall racing by his side started on another dribble.

Only the vilest ill-luck prevented us from taking the lead. Back to the inside-left the ball went when Vassall had drawn the defence, and Bridges literally hurled himself at the ball.

There was power behind Bridges' left foot, and this time the ball got the benefit of every ounce of it.

Straight as an arrow it sped for the far corner of the goal. It seemed impossible for the shot to be saved. It was not saved, but just as it appeared certain to enter the net the ball in some inexplicable fashion developed a "loft," and the end came with it smashing against the juncture of the upright and the cross-bar. Such was the force with which it hit the woodwork that it rebounded to beyond the penalty area.

Thrills were frequent— "three-a-penny" in McPhail's words.

Straight from that fortunate escape, Canaver's forwards came sharpshooting. Down the line the ball travelled, very beautiful—if disturbing—to see. Stanhope, beaten once, ran back to give his backs a hand. Over-anxious—who can tell what fears were rioting in his brain?—he stumbled, and when the Canaver's centre-forward was but fifteen yards from goal he was sprawling helpless in the mud.

Straightaway the forward shot—and the ball was like a brown streak. I scarcely dared look—and then a frenzied cheer set the blood tingling afresh.

'What a save!' cried someone. Although I had not looked myself, others had had more courage. And these had seen a very wonderful piece of goalkeeping; they had seen Merrick leap sideways at that flashing shot, just get to the ball, tip it into the air, catch it as it fell, slip sideways in order to avoid the mad charge of another Canaver's forward, and finally punt clear. When the crowd saw Birtles pat the hero heartily on the back, the wild cheers burst out afresh.

'I think we shall win now,' McPhail said gravely; 'before—well, I wasn't sure... Golly!' he added a second later in another tone, 'Geekie's out!'

There was a groan of agony in his voice—as well there might be. In trying to round the opposing left-half, Geekie, who had played so well so far, was heavily charged. No one thought anything about this until it was seen that our outside-right stayed on the ground instead of getting up.

Presently the word came that Geekie's ribs were damaged, and that he might not be able to play any more.

Of course, it was an accident—an intentional foul was almost unknown in Repington football—but fact remained that we were likely to be a man short in the second half—a calamitous happening. Then the half-time whistle went.

It would take me too long to describe in detail the progress of the second half of this palpitating duel. Let me content myself by sketching the main details before dealing with the nerve-tingling finish.

Geekie came back after ten minutes of the re-start. He was useless, however—or practically so—for he held his hand to his side when he ran, and was obviously in great pain. Stanhope spoke to him, but Geekie shook his head; so long as he could stand he was going to continue to do his bit. Foolish, you may say—but still rather splendid. If ever anyone had represented a forlorn hope at the commencement of that football season it had been Geekie, but faith and patience had fashioned him into an outside-right of rare ability. And Geekie was grateful.

But the crippling of Geekie had this effect upon the rest of the team; they re-doubled their efforts. Practising the sound strategy that attack was the best form of defence, Stanhope became a sixth forward as well as a half-back.

A spirit of greatness animated the side: with ten men and a cripple they kept the foe at bay. And Vassall, in this time of testing, became the greatest player on the field.

Time fled. Now there were but ten minutes to go.

Thrills still came at the rate of three a minute, even if there were no goals. Chief interest centred in the feud that was being waged in the middle of the field. Canaver's captain, realizing what magic Vassall carried in his football boots, had commanded his centre-half to shadow the elusive centre as closely as a prison warder. Canaver's had learned wisdom, and was allowing this stormy petrel no room to work his wiles. Directly the ball went in his direction the opposing defence concentrated on him.

Even so, he made one or two mesmeric runs, weaving a way through the serried ranks of the opposition; but his final shots were blocked, and no more goals would Tads' get this drab March day, it seemed.

Two minutes from the end, and in a last desperate attempt to defeat fate, Stanhope scraped the ball forward.

Canaver's captain clapped his hands in warning; but this time Vassall had swept past his football guardian; tapped the dropping ball into instant subjection, and had darted forward in a fast dribble. The three actions appeared to be done simultaneously, so swiftly was the movement initiated.

Thudding, hysterical cheers—and he was away on his last raid!

Clean down the centre of the field he raced, opponents pelting at his heels, but never able to stay his progress. We of the craning crowd saw him, feinting and swerving, beat man after man before heading straight for goal—

'Vassall!' came the exhorting cry, and again—' Vassall!'

He seemed to get fresh impetus as they shouted his name. He commanded the situation; he was like a great actor dominating a tremendously exciting scene —at least that was how it struck me. Leaving one of the Canaver's backs standing leaden-footed in the mud, he raced on.

'*Oh-h!*'

The cry of dismay came from us in a sudden burst. For we had seen him stumble whilst travelling at break-neck speed.

'*Vassall!*'

The shout now was jubilant. The clouds of doubt had been swept away; the forward had regained his balance; retrieved the ball from an opponent—and gone on!

With the excitement-crazed crowd still shouting his name, Vassall must have felt like a god. Had he dared to divert his mind he would have thought of us all standing on the touch-lines, our hearts in our mouths.

But he had to get that goal: it was the last chance he would have. For Tads' sake he must do it.

Espying an opening, he shot forward. There was a mist before his eyes, but he could see the goalkeeper hopping about like a cat on hot bricks.

Fellows, heavily breathing, were racing either side of him. They were trying to shoulder him off the ball. In front was the goalkeeper, bent double, hopping, hopping…

Suddenly, he saw the man leave his goal; he rushed forward in frantic haste, a human tornado.

Vassall knew this to be the testing time; knew that one false move now, one second's loss of nerve, would bring failure and bitter regret.

Calling on his aching limbs, he made a desperate spurt, the nervous kids in the crowd raised their hands to shield their gaze, for a collision between the rushing goalkeeper and forward seemed inevitable.

Some did not shudder; this was a man's game and men were playing it. For their hardihood they saw a piece of football craft which deserved to pass into history.

We saw Vassall lift the ball over the head of the oncoming goalkeeper, swerve past to avoid the charge which the other meant to give him, race ahead, regain the ball, and dribble it fiercely into the empty goal. He was travelling at such a pace that only the net stopped his headlong flight.

There was no time to re-start the game. But who wanted the game re-started? Any football after that breath-taking goal would have been an anti-climax. Canaver's partisans joined with Tads' supporters in acclamation, and all the world seemed to go mad.

So the great game died amidst a riot of enthusiasm. As he walked from that field of mud and glory, Vassall looked like one who has fulfilled his destiny.

Dog-weary and sated, aching in every limb, as he was throbbing in every nerve, his mud-stained lips parted in an irresistibly happy smile.

For he had not only won the cup for Tads', but had justified the faith which had nerved him to the task.

D 484

THIS WAS A MAN'S GAME

167

CHAPTER XXXIII

The Secret

That night all the seniors who took an interest in football—including Manners, the Captain of Repington, and Willoughby, the Skipper of Canaver's—came to Stanhope's study to offer congratulations. It was a memorable gathering.

Everyone was frankly delighted—even the leader of Canaver's defeated host—and Stanhope was looking overwhelmed when Tads entered.

As usual he was greeted with acclamation.

'Congratulations, sir!' said Canaver's skipper sportingly.

'Thank you, Willoughby.'

'By the way, sir, it's an extraordinary thing about Vassall,' went on the latter.

There was a twinkle in Tads' eyes as he replied: 'What's an extraordinary thing, Willoughby?'

'Why, a fellow pulling out such a game as he did to-day—especially after being a funk-shy.'

'Yes, it is rather extraordinary,' conceded the master. He looked round the group of interested faces. 'If you fellows would like to hear it, I will tell you the story,' he said. 'Vassall is cured, so he won't mind—but, all the same, I should like you chaps to keep it more or less to yourselves.'

All signified consent by nodding; and all became interested.

'Vassall's father, as all of you are aware,' started Tads, 'was a famous old Rep. He was the finest centre-forward that the school has ever had. He went on to Oxford, got his Blue and turned out for the Corinthians. Whilst with Corinth he played for England and gained International fame. You all know that, but there's no harm in reminding you of the facts; they have a bearing on my story.

'What you fellows—or, at least not all of you—don't know is that Vassall senior died practically on the football field. He was playing for the

Corinthians against Queen's Park, when he got a kick on the head. It was the purest accident, of course, but he died as the result of it.

'You can imagine what a terrible shock it was to his wife—our Vassall's mother. It was not to be wondered at, perhaps, that she hated football—the very mention of the game. And she brought her son up to fear the game—and made him promise that he would never play.

'This was the position when our Vassall came to Repington. He wouldn't have come to the shop at all but for his uncle, who talked Mrs. Vassall over in the matter. Mrs. Vassall knew that if her boy came to the school, which his father had made famous through his football playing, it would be difficult for him to keep his promise.

'Vassall found it impossible. The love for the game had always been dormant within him, although he did not know it, and when he came to the shop he felt, of course, that he simply had to play.

'But—and it is a big "but"—when he went on the field he found his mind was full of the things he had heard his mother tell him so often. He was afraid of getting hurt and thus bringing grief to the mother who was so fond of him. That was why Vassall funked—partly because he had been trained, as you may say, to be afraid of playing football, and partly because he knew that if he did get injured and his mother got to hear about it she would be caused acute distress. I hope you fellows can understand.'

'Of course, sir,' said Stanhope, and some of the others nodded. Even the minority who weren't able fully to grasp the situation as Tads had outlined it looked sympathetic.

'Vassall had a streak. But it was a streak caused by training and environment; it was not of his own making. To show that he wasn't a funk he took up boxing. He hoped to learn through boxing how to overcome his disability on the football field.

'He did well at boxing—how well you fellows know. But still he funked at football. The knowledge hurt him. He brooded over it, as such a decent chap naturally would do. He wanted to do his bit for his house and for the shop.

'I was keen to help him; Watney, Stanhope, Manners—we were all keen to help him. But in the end he helped himself.

'It was in the match against the team of Old Reps. You remember how the Old Boys came a man short? You remember that Vassall took this man's place at centre-forward and played a clinking game? You remember how he didn't show a sign of funking through-out the match?'

'Yes—yes, sir,' came the excited chorus.

'Well, two factors—one reacting on the other—caused the change. Sometime before Mr. Laidlay—Gilbert Laidlay—the night that he told us about the Corinthians' Cup, as a matter of fact—had had a talk with Vassall about the boy's funking. He had told him that it rested with himself, but that if he used his will-power it would probably wear off in time. Well, this thought must have been working away in Vassall's mind, and knowing that he would play in front of Laidlay himself that afternoon did wonders. There was something else, too; before the match Laidlay took him aside, and, realizing how desperately keen Vassall was on making good, said that if the wish to funk came—as undoubtedly it would—he (Vassall) must think of his father. I have no doubt that the spirit of his dead father helped Vassall considerably that afternoon.

'The human will can work wonders,' continued Tads, very seriously, 'and we have had an example in the case of Vassall. He has overcome a tremendous weakness by sheer will-power, and turned it into a strength. He will never funk again. Vassall still has his streak—but I think you fellows will agree it is a streak of greatness; inevitably, in my opinion, he is destined to take his father's place as England's centre-forward!'

How the cheers volleyed and thundered!

I have come to the end of my tale. The rest is a series of vivid but fleeting impressions—the parting from Stanhope, most beloved of skippers; the scene when Gilbert Laidlay, who had come down especially for the occasion, handed him, as Captain of Tads', the Corinthians' Cup; the frantic burst of applause which greeted the name "Vassall" when Stanhope, in his brief reply, said that whilst all the team had done their share, the centre-forward had done more than his share.

And the final impression of all: Vassall and Birtles getting into the same carriage at the railway station bound for Merrywood, laughing and joking—the best of friends.

McPhail—of course—had the last word.

'To see those fellows together almost restores my faith in human nature,' he said.

Dear Reader

If you thought this book was at least mildly entertaining, it would be really appreciated if you could do a quick review on Amazon, Goodreads or other online sites you use. Just a word or two would be great. 1889 Books is a small-scale undertaking so word of mouth is vital to letting readers know about it.

You can sign up for news and offers at www.1889books.co.uk, such as a free e-book of my first novel *The Evergreen in Red and White* set in Sheffield in 1897/98, based on the true story of Rabbi Howell, the first Romani international footballer.

I have published several other great books with a football theme including another Sydner Horler classic, *The Great Game,* and the superb *Ghosts of Inchmery Road* by Mat Guy.